Lost in Us

Layla Hagen

Dear Reader,
If you would like to receive news about my upcoming books, sales and giveaways, please sign up for my author mailing list HERE: http://laylahagen.com/mailing-list-sign-up/

Published by Layla Hagen

This edition contains the re-edited version of Lost in Us that was published in 2015.

CHAPTER ONE

There are three reasons tequila is my new favorite drink.

One: my ex-boyfriend hates it.

Two: downing a shot looks way sexier than sipping my usual Sprite.

Three: it might give me the courage to do something my ex-boyfriend would hate even more than tequila—getting myself a rebound.

"You need someone hot, hot, hot," my best friend Jess says, plunking her glass on the sleek counter and beckoning the bartender to prepare another round.

I grimace as the last drops of liquor burn my throat. "Define hot."

"Tall, tan, six-pack." She spins on her bar stool, turning toward the buzzing room.

"Every polo player at Stanford fits that

description," I say.

"Precisely."

She bursts into a torrent of giggles that makes me wonder if I shouldn't accidentally-on- purpose knock over the fresh round of shots the bartender sets in front of me, or my big night might just end up with me carrying an incoherent Jess to our apartment, as usual.

"Stanford's entire team is here. Have your pick, Serena."

I twirl around, facing a sea of people. Of course the entire team is here. Almost every Stanford student is here tonight. Who would miss the first bash of the spring quarter? For Jess and me, it's the last first bash ever, since we are graduating in a few months. I push my chest forward, the way Jess does it, fully aware that I won't have nearly the same effect she has. My black tank top, which she insisted I wear, doesn't do me justice, revealing far too much of my barely-there cleavage, despite the definitely-there Victoria's Secret push-up bra.

Jess twirls a blonde strand of her hair between her fingers, looking around with a confidence that can be neither replicated nor simulated. I take a deep breath and push the curtain of my black hair behind my shoulder. One look at the polo team and I know this was a bad, bad idea. The prospect of *talking* to one of those over-tanned giants, let alone flirting, has me hyperventilating. I don't know how to flirt. Last time I did it I was a high school junior, and I sucked at it. Also, I thought I would never have to do it again. But six years later, Michael decided his Australian coworker's seemingly endless legs were not to be resisted anymore, so here I am, a college senior, facing my most daunting exam yet.

I better not fail.

Yet as the number of mind-blowing, gorgeous girls floating around the players increases by the second, all vying for their attention, I dearly wish I could escape and cuddle in my bed, surrounded by mountains of Toblerone chocolate, watching *The Lord of the Rings* extended edition for the seventh time in three weeks.

I do a quick mental assessment of the probability of escaping without Jess catching on. It's not good. Besides, she *will* need me to carry her home, so I'd better not leave her alone. I almost start designing a plan to convince her to bolt together, when someone catches my attention.

He's tall, with dark, messy hair. Judging by the lavish gazes that the blonde at the next table and the redhead on his right throw him, I'm not imaging his perfectly toned chest and arms. On a hotness scale from one to ten, I'd put him between fifteen and sixteen.

I lean in to Jess and say in a low voice, "I bet he fits your hotness requirements."

She follows my gaze and starts giggling again. "James Cohen?"

"You know him?" *Please don't say you dated him. Please don't.*

"I've read an article about him. He looks hotter than the feature's picture. You of all people must have heard of him, too," she teases.

"The name does sound familiar," I admit, trying to hide my relief. I wrack my brain for a few seconds. And then it hits me. "Oh yeah, Stanford's golden boy. Every professor in my economics classes mentions him at least once a month. The poster child for successful serial entrepreneurs."

"Serial womanizers more likely," Jess smirks as he bends to the redhead, whispering something in her ear, sliding his hand playfully down her back. For some reason, the sight of them erases any desire to keep looking for potential prey, so I swirl on my stool back to the bar.

"He graduated a few years ago. What's he doing in a student bar?" I ask.

"Alumni sometimes come to semester opening parties," Jess says with a shrug. "Right. I need to pee." She springs from her stool, swaying when her feet reach the floor.

"Do you want me to come with you?" I ask at

once.

"No, no, I'm fine. I guess I shouldn't have drunk those cocktails before you arrived."

"That's right, you shouldn't have."

"But the guy buying them was so cute," she calls over her shoulder. I grimace as she stumbles into a couple on her way to the restroom.

I turn my attention to the two tequila shots in front of me, and open my mouth to tell the bartender we won't be having them after all, when a voice says, "I'd recommend you try it with orange slices and cinnamon."

"Excuse me?"

I look sideways and almost fall of my seat. It's *him*. And up close, it's obvious I gave him far too few points. His striking blue eyes and full lips, curled in a deliciously conceited smile, earn him at least a twenty on that hotness scale.

"Tequila," he points at the two glasses. "It tastes much better with orange and cinnamon than lemon and salt."

"Thanks for the tip." I flash my teeth in the hope they'll detract his attention from my plunging neckline, though I never heard of teeth trumping boobs.

"Have we met?"

"Umm... " I'm one hundred percent sure we haven't or I would remember, but I'm perfectly willing to pretend we have met if it means he'll linger here a little longer.

"We have," he says, recognition lighting up his face. "You were a mentor for the national math contest last year, weren't you?"

Damn. Of the myriad of rules Jess recited to me concerning flirting and dating, one in particular stands out: never show my nerdy side. And there are very few things nerdier than being a mentor in a math contest. Especially since only previous winners are allowed to mentor. In my defense, he was the one who brought it up. I make a mental note not to mention my part-time bookkeeping job. No need to add the boring tag, in addition to the nerd one.

"Yep, that's right."

"I was at the award ceremony," he says, "as a sponsor."

That would explain why I don't remember him, even though there weren't more than a dozen people there: teachers, parents, and sponsors. The award ceremony took place the day before the seven-year anniversary of my sister's death. I wasn't paying much attention to anything that week.

He frowns. "Your speech was very intense."

I stare at him, not sure if he's pulling my leg or not. That must have been the most horrid speech in history. I'd completely forgotten everything I'd prepared, so I started rambling wildly when my turn came. I can't remember one word I said, but I must have made an impression if he still remembers me.

"I'm James, by the way."

"I know. I mean… I've heard of you," I mumble, suddenly feeling very hot.

He seems completely unsurprised.

"I'm Serena McLewis."

"So, Serena…" he pronounces my name slowly, as if the three syllables would hide some kind of secret he's hoping to uncover. My name in his mouth gives me goose bumps all over my arms. I hope he doesn't notice them. "Let me guess, you're a math major?"

"Nope. Economics and computer science."

"Perfect combination. I had the same." He winks. "I could use someone smart like you in my company."

Just my luck. Other girls get a free drink, or a one-night stand. I get a job offer. Pity that's the last thing I want from him.

"Sorry, not interested," I say, hoping I don't sound too disappointed.

He leans forward, and his hand accidentally brushes mine. Gently, passing. But it's enough to send a torrent of shivers down my spine.

"And why is that?"

I try hard to come up with something, anything, but his warm breath on my cheeks wipes any thought other than the fact that his lips are far closer to me than they should be. His delicious scent—ocean and musk—makes my task so much harder.

He takes pity on me and leans back, his smirk more pronounced than ever as he scans me from head to foot.

"Are you doing anything tomorrow?" he asks.

A burning sensation starts forming in my chest and I don't know if it's panic or excitement, but I try to play cool, the way Jess always said I should.

"Of course, it's Saturday."

"Can you get out of it?"

I sound braver than I feel when I answer, "Depends on what you have in mind."

"Where do you live?" he muses.

Normally, a stranger asking for my address would not elicit any reaction from me except running in the opposite direction, while seriously considering calling the police. On second thought, I might add a punch for good measure before bolting. Yet as I stand here before him, watching his eyes trace the contour of my lips, all I can think is that I'm sorry I haven't had one more tequila. Then I might have enough courage to give him a kiss. As it is, I'll have to be content with giving him my address. I become conscious that I'm biting my lower lip and stop immediately. I lean over the bar and grab a napkin, then rummage in the tiny bag Jess lent me for a pen. I write my address on the napkin.

He glances at it once, picks it up and tucks it in the pocket of his jeans. "I know where that is. I'll have someone pick you up tomorrow at three."

"To go *where*?"

"What fun would that be if I told you?" he teases.

"You want me to get in a car with a stranger and trust him to take me to some place I don't know?"

He narrows his eyes. "Not very adventurous, are you?"

Ouch.

I would dismiss this as a poor attempt to provoke me, if Jess wouldn't tell me the same thing at least twice a day. Someone else used to tell me that as well. I never thought he really meant it until he announced that not only was he leaving me for the Aussie blonde but that he'd quit his job and was going backpacking with her through Europe and living life one day at a time.

I put on what I hope is a very pro-adventure smile. "How am I supposed to know how to dress if I don't know where I'm going?"

He bites his lip and leans in whispering, "I'll give you a hint. It's not a job interview."

"You don't even know me."

"I'd love to get to know you," he says in a raspy, seductive voice that sends delicious tingles all over my body.

For a wonderful, wonderful second, in which his blue eyes—a few shades darker than when I first noticed them—bore into mine, I think he might close the distance and kiss me.

But then he straightens up and frowns at something behind me. "I think your friend needs help."

I whirl around in a heartbeat, and find Jess leaning on a tall, blond guy, her arms tight around his neck, something that usually makes guys pretty happy. Not this one. He's using both arms in his attempt to shake her off.

"See you tomorrow, Serena," James whispers in my ear, making the hair at the nape of my neck stand up. I don't need to turn to know he's gone. I remain on my seat for a few more seconds, breathing in the last lingering wisps of his scent, then shove the glasses to the bartender, smiling apologetically, and head straight toward Jess.

"I'll take this from here."

"Thank God," the guy says, his voice flooded with relief as I unhitch Jess's arms from his neck.

He vanishes the second I free him.

"That went well," Jess giggles in my ear. And apparently she absolutely has to hang from someone's neck tonight, because she heaves her arms around mine so forcefully I'm positive I'll have giant bruises on both sides of my neck tomorrow.

"What are you talking about?" I say, trying hard to steer us both toward the door.

"You and hot guy. You really should work on your expression, though."

"What about my expression?"

She laughs. "You looked like you were ready to jump in bed with him."

"That's not true," I say indignantly, stopping mid-stride.

"Oh trust me, it is. And by the way, he's staring at us right now so keep moving if you don't want him to see me throwing up on you."

CHAPTER TWO

"**S**top making so much noise," Jess complains, pulling the sheet over her head.

"It's not my fault you couldn't make it to your room last night," I say, continuing to search for something suitable to wear.

It actually *is* my fault. When we arrived from the club last night I decided I couldn't possibly carry her all the way to her room, so I put her to bed in my room instead. I slept in her bed, something I regret more with each second. Her bedroom is the only place in our apartment where I couldn't ban smoking, and now it smells worse than a sports bar. I poured half a bottle of shampoo in my hair this morning, but I swear I can still smell smoke under the peach and melon fragrance.

"What do you think?" I ask, holding out a white strapless dress.

A deep snore is my only answer. I sigh and slip into the dress. It'll do. I'm not changing yet again. I step in front of the mirror, and as I swirl, I can't help questioning my sanity. Now that the last effects of the tequila have vanished, I am more and more convinced that I imagined the entire conversation last night. Not convinced enough though, or I wouldn't have spent the past two hours trying on almost every single dress I own. I decide it's time to walk away from my closet as the urge to try another one kicks in. I turn my attention to the wall opposite my bed instead and smile. Like Jess's room, mine too is a testament to the vices of its owner.

Chocolate, books, and DVDs.

An entire wall of them.

There are five shelves on the wall, the top three occupied with books and DVDs and the remaining two with chocolate boxes. Fancy wooden or metal boxes, or just regular plastic ones—I don't discriminate. Most boxes and cartons are empty, but I keep them because they make a nice decoration.

For the first day since the break-up, my stomach isn't twisted in a painful knot, and I don't feel the overwhelming need to pick a DVD and one of the remaining untouched chocolate boxes, then hide under my covers. I could argue it's because Jess is in my bed, and I wouldn't return in hers for anything in the world, but I know that would be a lie.

There is another reason for my sudden optimism.

It's a silly reason.

An almost absurd reason.

One that makes my heart beat quicker and my face turn hot every time I think about it.

James Cohen.

I wonder if I should make Jess her beloved (and utterly ineffective) banana and kiwi hangover cure and leave it on the bedside table, but it's likely to go bad by the time she wakes up, and leaving it in the fridge will ensure she won't drink it. No, I'm sure she'll be asleep until I'm back. A rustling noise comes from the direction of the bed. As Jess resurfaces from under the sheets, a painful knot forms in my throat.

When she's asleep, she reminds me of my sister Kate. Their full lips and golden, silky locks are almost identical. She was four years older than me. She brimmed with life, every waking moment, and I adored her.

She adored me, too. She'd spend hours taking care of me, teaching me how to comb my hair so it would shine like hers (not that it ever did) or painting my nails in intricate motifs.

Then she'd disappear for days. With her friends. Boyfriend. Whomever. Her only yardstick for choosing them seemed to be the number of times they'd visited a police station. I could find her easily in the beginning, but later on, it sometimes took me an entire week to discover her whereabouts.

When I took her home, I'd be the one taking care of her. I'd wipe away her mascara, put tea bags on the dark circles under her eyes, and lay packs of ice on the pierced veins of her arms.

I take a deep breath and shake my head. Jess is not like Kate. After Kate passed away, Mum and Dad did something I will be eternally grateful for. They sent me away from London, our hometown. Even though it broke their heart, they did it. They sent me to live with Jess's family in San Francisco. My mum and Jess's mum had been best friends since kindergarten, and remained close even after Jess's mum moved across the ocean, to San Francisco, while mum remained in their native London. Starting fresh, far away from the city that held so many memories and so much guilt, was the best thing that could have happened to me. I stayed with Jess and her family throughout high school. I haven't returned to London at all. My parents fly here once a year to visit me.

I take one last look at Jess and smile before

leaving the room.

I check my phone while drinking my third cup of coffee today, seated in my second favorite place in our apartment after my bed—the couch. One message from Mum: *Dad and I are planting Langloisia today. Talk to you in the evening.*

I can't stop a chuckle. The idea of my parents gardening is something I still cannot get used to. Or rather, the idea of my dad gardening. Mum has always been in love with flowers. But she never had time for gardening, or anything else after her long hours at the design studio where she had worked as a seamstress.

My dad worked equally long hours on an assembly line. Three years ago he lost all ability to move his legs in a freak factory accident, and the firm offered him a nice settlement if he didn't take them to court. Mum decided to work from home on her own afterward so she could take care of him. Between her sewing and the settlement, they manage to scrape by. I plan to change that to a decent living as soon as I get a job. But the new arrangement has a positive side to it: they started having a lot of time to spend with each other. Somehow Mum convinced Dad they should dedicate most of that time to gardening.

Mum and Dad met in high school and started dating in their junior year. They married after graduation and have lived happily together ever since. Even during those horrible years with Kate, when life was hell for all four of us, their love never faltered.

Michael and I started dating in our junior year and I assumed happily ever after was a given for us. Guess not.

I glance at the clock. Still half an hour left. I toy with the idea of sending a few more job applications before I leave—an endeavor that has taken up countless nights and weekends lately. I decide against it. This is not the time to sink into the usual negativity about my future that inevitably follows the emailing of every batch of applications.

At five to three I'm in the parking lot in front of our building, next to Jess's fourth-hand (though she claims it's second-hand) Prius, carrying a brown cotton blazer on my left arm. Even though it's only mid-March, it's pleasantly warm.

I fiddle with the strap of my bag, trying to arrange it somehow so it won't cut into my shoulder anymore. There is no sign of anyone in the lot. As the minutes tick by, the irrational fear that last night was nothing but a wishful dream starts creeping back into my mind.

The fear dissipates at three o'clock sharp and nervous jitters replace it, as a white Range Rover makes its way through the lot, standing out in the sea of Priuses and Fords like a whale among baby dolphins.

It stops a few feet away from me.

A tall, slightly older man wearing a black suit steps out of the car. I'm surprised by the wave of disappointment that hits me. Though James said he would send someone to pick me up, I realize that I still hoped he'd show up, wearing that conceited smile of his.

"Ms. McLcwis?" thc man asks in an official tone.

I take a step forward. "You can call me Serena."

For some reason I didn't expect James Cohen, the founder of several high-tech and Internet ventures, the prime example of all things modern, to be employing a driver. One that wears a uniform at that.

"Peter Sullivan, at your service. I was sent by Mr. Cohen to pick you up." He opens the back door and gestures to me to get inside.

I nod and hop inside the car.

When Peter takes his place in the driver's seat I ask as casually as possible, "How long will the trip take?"

He starts the engine and drives onto the main street, and though I can only see his eyes in the mirror when he answers, I'm pretty sure he's trying very hard to stifle a laugh. "I was instructed not to give you any information that might disclose our destination."

I lean back, recognizing defeat. What is James playing at? What difference does it make whether I find out now or in half an hour?

But I don't find out in half an hour. Or in one hour. Three hours pass before we finally get off the highway. By that time I've bitten all my nails, and the thought of calling the police to notify them of my own kidnapping has passed through my mind at least half a dozen times.

I relax a bit as we enter a very wealthy residential area. To my left and right lie houses—palaces really, each more grandiose than the previous one.

But we don't stop in front of any of them. Peter drives by house after house, until the houses get farther apart, and finally fields replace them. It's a while before the first sign of civilization begins to appear: a fence. Behind it lies a neat garden, adorned with so many roses that it looks more like a nursery. There is no house in sight.

The car comes to a halt in front of the huge double gates. I still see no house behind them. My stomach gives a slight jolt when the gates open and we drive inside.

***

“Wow," I exclaim when the house finally comes into view. "Wow," I repeat as I stumble out of the car.

This isn't a house. It's the ultra-modern, almost futuristic version of a palace. Except for the ground floor, it seems to be made entirely of glass, with the odd wooden wall here and there. Its owners must be fascinated by square forms, because the entire building is an amalgam of smaller and larger cubes. At least, the part observable from here is. The place must be swarming with people, judging by the number of cars all around me.

"You are expected inside, Ms. McLewis," Peter says, obviously amused by my reaction.

"I am?" I ask in amazement and start walking with trembling steps toward the entrance.

I close my palm around the handle of the massive oak door and expect to have to put some energy into pushing it, but it opens effortlessly.

The moment I step inside, the simplicity of my white dress slaps me in the face. There are no words to describe how many levels of underdressed I am compared to the sleek, shiny surfaces and exquisite paintings on the walls, each with a picture light above it.

"Name," a deep voice calls, startling me. I turn

around and locate the source behind the door.

"Serena McLewis," I answer.

The man scans the long list he's holding, then continues to the next page. And the next page. I count four page turns. "You're not on the list."

Everything from his polished shoes to his perfectly knotted tie and his neatly gelled hair tells me he's not the type to let me in if I'm not on the list.

"James Cohen invited me."

He raises an eyebrow.

"You think I sneaked in?" I ask him incredulously.

His expression tells me that is exactly what he thinks. My casual, beach-appropriate dress isn't helping my case, either.

"Let her in, Loren," a young girl squeaks from the far end of the hallway, hurrying toward us. Loren instantly lowers the list and gestures me to proceed.

"I'm so sorry, I didn't have time to put you on the list," the girl says, looking genuinely distressed. As she comes closer, I realize she's not as young as I thought. Her round, dark eyes and the slight fullness of her face are misleading, but she must be at least seventeen. To my relief, she's wearing a robe. A beautiful one, made of silk, but a robe nonetheless.

"I'm Dani," she says.

She takes my hand before I get a chance to introduce myself and pulls me in the direction she came from. "We need to get you changed," she says. "You can't go to the party dressed like *this.*"

I stare at her black, unnaturally perfect curls, biting my lip. I know my dress isn't much, but coming from someone dressed in a robe, the comment seems a little off.

"What party?"

"Ooh. You're British." Her eyes widen with delight. "My brother didn't tell me that. And he clearly didn't tell you anything," she says, smirking and opens the door that marks the end of the hallway.

"James is your brother?" I ask blankly.

"I know, the similarities between us are astounding. I—"

The rest of her sentence gets lost in the sudden explosion of words and laughter filling the room in front of us. Two dozen women, most of them around my age, sit on a long row of chairs in front of a mirror that covers the entire wall. Behind each of them is a hairstylist, turning their hair into curls just as unnaturally perfect as Dani's. Three of the girls are fully dressed, and the mystery surrounding the party—or at least part of it—dissipates.

"It's a themed party," I say.

"Eighteenth century Venice." Dani winks. "My mother throws themed parties every year for charity. It's Venice this time. Let's get you a dress."

On the other side of the room are rows and rows of metal bars with clothes hangers holding long, festive chiffon and velvet dresses.

"I set some dresses aside for you," Dani calls over her shoulder as we make our way through the rows of dresses. "Let's look at those first, and if you don't like any you can look for something else. Unfortunately, there won't be time to have your hair done because my lovely brother sent Peter far too late to fetch you."

"No problem," I say, trying not to sound too relieved that I get to keep my hair as it is. "So, um… you live here with your parents?"

"Yep. James sometimes comes here on weekends. When he's not working," she says, rolling her eyes. "But I actually prefer it if he doesn't come here. Gives me an excuse to go down in San Jose."

Silicon Valley's capital. Where else could he live? Yet another mirrored wall marks the back of the room. Thankfully, there's no one in front of it. In the left corner is a small open wooden closet containing five dresses.

"Which one do you want to try on?" Dani claps her hands excitedly.

"The red one," I say without hesitation. In addition to being the prettiest dress I've ever seen, it's red. Red is my favorite color, but I don't wear it often. I don't know why, probably because I feel I attract too much attention whenever I wear it, something I'm not very comfortable with. But today—tonight, actually—is different. Wearing red seems like the right thing to do.

"It's perfect," I say when Dani holds the dress in front of her, faking a bow.

She giggles. "I'll help you with it, then you can help me with mine. I tried getting dressed on my own and nearly wanted to tear the damn thing apart."

To my confusion, Dani waits in front of me while I take my clothes off, completely unfazed by my discomfort. I discard my plain little white dress on the floor and pull the red one over my head as fast as possible—with Dani's help. She's right, doing it by myself would have been a nightmare. For all its beauty, it's so heavy I hope I won't have to do much more than sit at a table for the rest of the evening.

When we finally manage to get the red dress on, I face the mirror.

It looks even more beautiful than it did on the hanger. The long, bouffant skirt reminds me of the drawings in the storybooks I used to devour when I was little.

"What's your story?" Dani asks. I can see her frown in the mirror, as she concentrates on the monstrous task of pulling the laces through the more than fifty eyelets of the bodice.

"What do you mean?"

"How long have you and James known each other?"

"Um..." I take a moment to consider my words. If I tell her I just met him last night, she'll think—rightly so—that I must be insane to show up here. Pretending to know him well will backfire faster than Jess's car on a particularly bad day.

I go for a neutral, "We met recently."

Her eyebrows shoot up in surprise, and the thinnest rivulets of sweat ooze on my temples. What did he tell her about me? He must have told her something. But if he did, I need all the cunning in the world to find out what.

"So are you applying to Stanford?" I ask.

"God no. I've been admitted to Oxford," she says proudly, "to study English literature."

"Congrats," I say, slightly surprised. For some reason, I can't picture Dani, with her black hair and slightly tanned skin, in a place without sun. "I'm a fan of English literature, too."

For some reason, my comment brings a

particularly bright smile on her face. "You're one of the very few people who didn't cringe and suggest I take up medicine or law."

"Well, I think everyone has the right to study what they want. Jess, my best friend, is studying history."

Her delicate hands have almost finished lacing up the bodice. "Not everyone can be business freaks like you and my brother," she winks.

Aha. What else did he tell her about me?

"He's quite smart, your brother."

And *hot*. The word forms in my mind by itself, and I'm glad Dani is so preoccupied with the eyelets. My cheeks turn almost as red as the dress.

"Please don't let him know you think that. Won't help that pig headedness of his in the slightest."

I squelch the urge to laugh as best as I can, because she says this in such a solemn tone that I'm sure she'd be highly offended if I didn't take her seriously. There is a slightly awkward pause while she laces the very last eyelets, in which the only sound is a high-pitched laugh from one of the girls in front.

When she's done she takes a few steps back and looks at me approvingly. "You look beautiful."

"Your turn," I say. "Which dress is yours?"

She picks a white dress from the nearest metal

bar and hands it to me. I make a point of keeping my eyes on the beautiful white chiffon while she discards her robe. After a few painful minutes, I actually manage to get her in her equally heavy dress without ruining her hair. She turns around and I start on the eyelets. I'm halfway through them when an eerie harp tune comes from Dani's robe. She completely ignores it.

"I think that's your cell," I say tentatively.

"I know. It's probably my boyfriend, trying to make up for completely bolting last night," she says through gritted teeth.

I proceed with the eyelets in silence.

"Do you have a boyfriend?" she blurts.

"Yes. I mean no," I say, taken aback by the sudden turn of the conversation. "We broke up a few weeks ago."

"Oh. I'm sorry. How long had you been together?"

"Six years. You should really answer that. Or switch it off," I say, pretending not to notice her shocked glance in the mirror as the phone starts ringing yet again.

She bends and picks the phone from the pocket of her robe with a rather sour expression that turns to affectionate annoyance when she notices the name on the screen. It's not her boyfriend.

It's James.

She presses the phone to her ear. "Where's the fire?"

I don't hear anything more than a buzzing noise coming from her phone, but it's enough for my stomach to give a little jolt. I can't even fathom what it'll do when I actually *see* James.

"But I'm not ready," she protests when the buzzing noise stops.

I signal her in the mirror that I'm almost done.

"Okay, okay, I'll be there in a minute," she says, giving up and closing the phone.

"I need to go. Will you be okay on your own? Just stick to the girls, they know where the ballroom is. I'll find you there," she says and runs off. "Make sure to take a mask from the closet," she calls over her shoulder before disappearing altogether.

CHAPTER THREE

With nothing left to do, I pick up my white dress, bag, and her robe and put everything on a hanger, then walk to the closet and discover a set of black masks. I grab one and make my way to the front of the room, wondering if the laughter is becoming louder, or I'm just imagining it. One glance at the cup of champagne each girl is holding tells me I am not. There are only four girls left now, and they are all gathered in a circle.

"Someone get Dani's friend a cup," one of them says in a disturbingly high-pitched voice, forcibly reminding me of a lark.

"I'm fine," I say.

"Oh, right, she's not allowed to drink," a redhead who looks vaguely familiar giggles. It takes me a moment to realize they think I'm the same age as Dani, a school colleague of hers. For some reason, I don't want to correct that impression. I have a hunch they are the last people who should know who really invited me here.

Their next words confirm this very thought.

"I bet Sophie'll get some tonight," the lark says, applying another layer of red lipstick on her full lips.

"Why me?" Sophie, the one who cemented my underage status, says with fake indignation.

"Because you're the only one among us who hasn't," the girl next to her chuckles. She'd give any swimsuit model a run for her money. "And James's had an eye on you for some time."

"He had his chance last night and *nothing* happened," Sophie exclaims, as if she couldn't imagine anything more offensive. With a flash, I realize why she looks familiar. She was the redhead standing next to James last night. I withhold a smile as an unnatural sense of triumph fills me at Sophie's indignation.

"Maybe it's your turn again," Sophie continues, eying the lark. "You used to hook up with him."

I guess Jess's womanizer comment deserved more credit than I gave it. I take a quick look at every girl. Whether redhead or blonde, full-lipped or not, their one common denominator seems to be that they're all drop-dead gorgeous.

The lark leans back in her chair, twirling one

dark brown lock around her fingers. "For old times' sake? Maybe," she replies, grinning with satisfaction. "Though I must say I found him much sexier in his rebel days."

I'm dying to know more details about those rebel days, but the lark is the last person I'd ask.

Sophie just stares at her.

I wonder how long it would take them to jump at each other's throats if there wasn't an actual law punishing them. Funny how they immediately thought I was a high school girl. Probably because they never outgrew that phase. I clutch my mask forcefully and exit the room, wishing more than ever that Jess were here or that I was home. What was I thinking? What was James thinking? Why did he invite me here? He's already got a group of desperate hyenas to choose from.

There are less than a hundred feet between the front door and me. Loren is still there, guarding it, but I'm pretty sure he won't try to stop me from leaving. The taxi back home would cost me a week's salary, but right now, that doesn't sound half bad.

And yet I don't move one inch from my frozen position against the door. There's something rooting me to the spot. Something that tells me this isn't the time to chicken out and flee.

I unhitch myself from the door and put the

mask on just as the hyenas burst out of the room. They, too, are wearing masks.

"There you are," Sophie giggles. "We were afraid we lost you."

The lark opens a door to a hall that looks as long as this one and the four of them walk inside. Sophie steps on her own dress and stumbles forward, nearly knocking the other girls over. As she bursts into yet another torrent of giggles, under the disdainful look of the lark, I make a mental note to get lost among the other guests as fast as possible.

***

"**W**ow," I exclaim for the third time tonight when we enter the ballroom.

A high glass arch spans above us, contrasting with the house's cubic form. It also contrasts with the classical dresses and tuxedos in a whimsical, almost eerie way. There must be more than a hundred people here, not including the orchestra. Finding Dani among the sea of masked men and women won't be an easy task, though there aren't many white dresses in sight. I step away from the hyenas as fast as possible, hoping the mask on my face and the champagne in their blood are a good enough camouflage.

I stand on my toes and try to spot Dani in the

crowd, something that becomes increasingly difficult because everyone is regrouping along the edges of the dance floor. I give up trying to advance when I'm so squeezed in between a middle-aged couple that I can barely breathe. The woman must have spilled an entire bottle of a nauseating sweet perfume on herself.

"Red suits you," a voice calls behind me. I'm suddenly very grateful for being squeezed in, because my knees seem to have turned weak. But my relief only lasts for a few seconds, because the music starts and everyone around me disperses, moving to the dance floor.

When he finally comes into view, my breath is cut short. There is something about seeing his beautiful blue eyes behind a mask that makes every inch of my skin burn.

So it wasn't the tequila last night.

"Dance?" He extends his hand.

"I can't dance." Out of the corner of my eye I see the lark watching us, crestfallen.

"That makes two of us," he says, though unlike me, he doesn't sound panicked in the slightest. I really can't dance. Especially not waltz. But he doesn't lower his hand, and instead of protesting further, I raise my hand and place it in his. As if in slow motion I see him putting his other arm around my waist, and pulling me so close to him that I feel his every breath against my skin. This doesn't help the burning sensation at all.

"You came," he says and his lips curve into last night's same conceited smile.

"I make a habit of honoring my invitations." I bite my lip and look away, fixing my gaze on the highest point of the glass arch.

"Did you and your friend arrive home safely last night?"

"If safely includes Jess throwing up twice on the way home, then yes."

"Quite a party girl, your friend," he says appreciatively.

"What makes you think I'm not one?" I regret the question instantly. Thinking that a former math whiz kid isn't the most hardcore party girl at Stanford is not an absurd conclusion to draw. But his answer takes me by complete surprise.

"Having a steady boyfriend usually means you spend your free evenings and weekends ... otherwise."

"You asked Dani to spy on me?"

"Of course not. I just know how to get the info I need from her."

"What happened to old-fashioned questioning?"

"It's old-fashioned," he answers with a smirk. "I like to consider myself modern."

"Make that lazy and sneaky." I finally unhitch

my gaze from the ceiling and look him in the eyes again.

He tightens his grip on my waist. "Fine. Tell me three things about you."

I try to put on my most serious look. "I grew up in London and San Francisco, used to play volleyball in a minor league, and want to work in investment banking." Did he really think I'll make it easy for him?

"Let me rephrase," he smirks. "Tell me three things about you I won't find in your CV. Your biggest dream."

The next sentence rolls out of my mouth despite my firm resolution to torment him by not really telling him anything about me. Especially not the weird things.

"Biggest dream: finding a way to eat a lot of chocolate and not put on weight. I love chocolate, and fantasy books and movies. I could stay indoors for weeks just reading and watching moves. As long as I have chocolate, of course."

He warm and heartfelt laughter. He's also loud.

"Your turn," I say, in an attempt to stop him, because we are attracting less-than-friendly stares from the couples around us. "Stop laughing like a maniac and tell me three things about yourself. Three fears."

He laughs for a few more seconds before

assuming a solemn face.

"I hate snakes and always keep a light on when I sleep. I'm also not a fan of commitment."

"So I've heard," I say, trying—and failing—to keep my voice steady.

"I wanted to make sure you know it from me," he says in a soft voice. "That's very considerate of you."

I feel like such a fool.

"I saw how you were looking at me in that bar," he whispers with urgency.

Crap, so Jess wasn't exaggerating. I do my best to put on the poker face she mimicked on our way home, then I remember I have a mask on anyway.

"Why did you invite me here?"

"Why did you come?" he asks, and there is a slight uneasiness in his voice.

"Because you invited me," I answer as sardonically as possible.

"I was curious," he says quietly.

I don't have a chance to find out what he was curious about, because the song ends, and the crowd moves, separating us. James takes a step in my direction, but an elderly man intercepts him, pulling him to one side for a conversation. He looks at me, but I shrug, mouthing "later", then turn and start walking as fast as possible through the sea of people.

When I reach the bar, I collide with someone so violently that I lose my balance. I close my eyes and grit my teeth in preparation for my impending clash with the parquet.

A sharp pain in my left arm tells me someone caught me in my free fall. The guy I collided with helps me get back on my feet. Wow. His eyes are just like James's, and so is his lopsided smile. It doesn't have that conceited, almost insolent air James's smile has, but the full lips and very fine dimple in his chin are identical.

"So sorry. Are you all right?"

He's English.

"Are you related to… Ja—the Cohens?" I say, biting my lip.

He looks taken aback for a moment, then his smile widens. "You're English. What a nice surprise. To answer your question, yes, my mother, Lady Catherine, and Lady Beatrix Cohen are sisters," he says in a formal tone that doesn't match his smile. "That makes me a first cousin to James and Dani. Of course, the paternal side of my family might also be of interest for you. Astounding pedigree. I'm two-hundred-forty-sixth in line for the British throne," he finishes, and I crack up.

"Not bragging about that again, Parker?" Dani

says, appearing at Parker's side out of nowhere.

"Just using everything in my arsenal to impress the fair lady here—"

"Serena," I say.

"Serena, in the hope she'll forgive me for knocking her over in the most unceremonious way."

Dani and I both burst out laughing.

"Are you okay?" she asks.

"Of course she is," Parker says. "If she isn't, she will be in a few minutes. There's nothing a gin and tonic can't remedy." He signals the bartender to make one.

"Can you get me one too?" Dani says, looking at him with hope.

Parker cocks a brow. "You're too young." He orders her something non-alcoholic instead. Then he puts one arm around her shoulders affectionately and the other one around mine as we watch the bartender make the drinks. "So, how come you never introduced me to your adorable friend before?"

"She didn't know her until today," a voice says from behind us.

Parker withdraws his arm. He and Dani turn around, but I take my time. I wait for the bartender to hand me the drink, take a sip, and only then follow suit. I find James's gaze fixed on me.

"Then I can blame you for not introducing us earlier," Parker jokes.

"Indeed," James says without taking his eyes off me. "Dani, I hope the drink behind you is for someone else."

A wave of warmth surges through me at such a blatant display of overprotectiveness toward his sister while Dani, understandably, scoffs.

"Would you mind if we finish our conversation?" James asks me.

"Sure," I say and follow him. He leads me to a small room behind the bar. It's filled with empty tables and cabinets carrying every imaginable type of glass and porcelain plates, and we're alone.

"I'm sorry we were interrupted."

"So, James. You were about to tell me why you invited me here. You said you were curious."

"You intrigue me. I wanted a chance to talk. This seemed like a good place to start."

"Well, this place is fascinating. I love the dress, and the theme." I smile, feeling butterflies in my stomach. Oh, God, he's so close, and he's moving even closer.

"I'm glad you accepted the invitation."

"I thought it was time to do something a bit reckless."

He swallows. "How reckless?"

He moves even closer, pushing me against one of the empty tables, putting his hands on my waist. His intoxicating ocean-and-musk scent invades my senses as every inch of his body is glued to mine. He breathes heavily against my neck, and each warm breath of his against my skin sends shudders through my body. I think I'm trembling, but I can't be sure. The only thing I am sure of is I don't want him to step away.

He doesn't step away. Instead, he takes off both our masks and kisses me.

Now I know why I came. For this. For the touch of his lips and the stroke of his strong, warm hands. One of his hands is still on my waist, the other one is on my thigh, furiously pulling up the fabric, until it reaches my skin. We both moan at the same time.

And then, just as suddenly as he started it, he stops the kiss and pulls away his hand, allowing the fabric to cover me again.

"Do you want to leave?" he mutters in my ear in a low voice.

"What?" I ask in alarm. Of all the things I want right now, leaving is not among them. "No."

He distances himself from me, just enough to be able to look me in the eyes. And I thought they were dark while we were dancing! That was nothing compared to the deep dark blue they are now.

"Are you sure?"

"Do *you* want me to leave, but don't know how to say it?"

"God, no," he says, digging his fingers deeper into my waist. "I told you I want to talk. Except now...instead of talking, I want to do dirty and delicious things to you, Serena."

No one has ever spoken to me this way, and my entire body reacts to it—especially my intimate spots.

"I won't say no," I whisper, suddenly feeling bold. I've never felt bold, but I like the change. I feel like I'm taking control.

"You just ended a long relationship," he says.

"Maybe I want to try something different," I say and his eyebrows shoot up.

"You won't—"

I lean forward and kiss him without giving him the chance to utter one reason that could change my mind. I don't even want to think this through. I want to have fun and be reckless, just for once.

He gasps for breath a few seconds later and I feel his conceited smile form against my lips as he says, "Let's get out of here."

He grabs my hand and opens the door and e step into a hallway similar to the one at the entrance, except there are no paintings in this one, and there are fewer doors.

He opens the door directly in front of us and pulls me in, flattening me against the door as soon as he closes it. We're in a library.

"Have you changed your mind?" He passes his thumb gently over my lips.

"No."

"Good." He leans in and starts perusing my neck with his lips, sending delicious little tingles down my spine. "Because I want you so badly."

A soft moan escapes my lips, triggered by his confession. His whole body expresses a craving that mirrors mine.

He covers my mouth with a kiss, an even more hungry and passionate kiss than the ones before it. His hands travel up my back and the slightest spasm of panic shakes me when he unceremoniously rips the eyelets apart, allowing my dress to fall to the ground, leaving me completely naked except for my panties. One second later, they land on the floor as well.

He steps back. His eyes travel slowly over my body, the blue in them getting darker and darker by the second. When they reach my chest I automatically move my hand in an attempt to cover my minuscule boobs, but he stops me midway and wraps me in his arms.

"You are so beautiful, Serena," he says in a low, raspy voice before kissing me again.

My desperate hands search for the buttons of his shirt, and I start undoing them one by one. I feel eighteen again, preparing for my first time. In many ways it is a first and it's even more nerve-wracking than the *real* first time. There was at least a bed involved, and a guy I had been dating for two years.

I press my fingers into his skin the second his shirt comes off, my touch leaving red marks on his perfectly toned body. *God, he's hot.*

He lifts me in his arms and I wrap my legs around him as he carries me around, never ceasing to kiss him, never ceasing to touch him.

A spasm of panic returns as he places me on my back on the leather couch and leans over me.

"You're nervous," he whispers in my ear.

"A bit." I have no doubt the tremble in my voice reveals just how nervous I am. "You have an unfair advantage over me," I point to his pants.

"You think?" he asks and presses himself to me. Feeling his erection against my bare midriff melts away my worries. Desire replaces every thought.

I unbuckle his belt as clumsily as I unbuttoned his shirt and take off his pants and boxer briefs at the same time. And then I touch him.

He is huge. Really huge.

"Fuck," he says in a husky voice, lowering his fingers to my thighs.

He bends over to one side, searching for something in the pocket of his trousers, taking out a condom.

I didn't stop taking birth control pills after breaking up with Michael, but say nothing. Given that I barely know him, using a condom is a good idea.

He places it between my breasts and commands, "Put it on."

I don't wait to be told again and rip off the cover with trembling hands. I look him in the eyes as I roll the thin condom over his erection, watching as his perfect face contorts in spasms of pleasure and frustration. It gives me immense pleasure to know I'm causing it. I arch my back, seeking to cut our prelude short.

"Not so fast," he teases and starts kissing my ear, descending painfully slowly on my neck and then my breasts. His tongue plays around one of my nipples while his fingers touch my sex in a teasing manner.

"James, please," I beg when the tension in my body becomes almost painful.

The gentle touch disappears as he presses his palm over my clit and moves in circles over and over again, sending hot and cold spasms through my body.

I cannot control my moans and pleas or the wildness as I dig my nails into his back.

"I want you to come," he whispers in my ear.

And I do.

Hard.

He covers my mouth with a kiss as my body succumbs to bliss. I barely recover my breath when he thrusts inside me, filling me completely.

"Fuck, Serena," he moans and pulls my head into another kiss. I pick up his rhythm and move my hips against his faster and faster, in a wild dance that has me sweating and moaning. But no matter how fast we move, it isn't fast enough. It isn't hard enough. I want faster. I want more. I want everything.

The spasms start again when I feel him growing, his furious breath intensifying by the second.

"Fuck," he groans in my ear as the blissful explosion overtakes me again. Between my uncontrollable shaking and moaning, I hear him come too.

It takes a while before my breathing returns to its normal pattern and I can form clear thoughts again. James is still over me, his head buried in my neck. His breathing too, is calm and regular now, but he pulled out of me. He slides over to one side and sits up on an elbow. His face contorts in a grimace and I immediately see why. There are four deep scratches on his left shoulder.

"You're a little beast," he teases, looking amused.

"You seemed to like it," I say, avoiding his gaze, feeling ashamed. He makes me say and do things I never did before… like scratching and biting.

"I never said I didn't," he says softly. "Did you like it? You're the important one."

I nod and turn to look him in the eyes. They are so bright now. I wonder if I'll ever have the opportunity to see them turn dark again, or if this was our one and only time together. His next move makes me think it's the latter. He gets up and pulls on his trousers in a heartbeat then disappears from my view only to return with my red dress a few seconds later.

"We're returning to the party?"

He takes my hand and helps me get up, then wraps me in his arms, holding me against his still damp body.

"Not yet. Too many people there. I want to spend a little more time with you. I also want your phone number."

"Oh, sure." He takes his phone out of my pocket, and I dictate my number. "So…what now?"

"There are thirty-seven rooms in this house," he

says with a delicious smile. "How about a tour?"

CHAPTER FOUR

"**I** can't believe you had sex with him," Jess says one week later for what must be the hundredth time. She drops her copy of the *Sixteenth Century Relics* on the coffee table and stares at me, then picks up her tablet, her attention focused on me.

Maybe it's time to change tactics. I've brushed off every single one of her previous questioning attempts with a laconic *I don't want to talk about it*, but she still isn't showing signs of wanting to let go of the matter.

"Isn't that the purpose of a rebound?" I ask.

"For normal people, yes," Jess says, looking both pleased and alarmed that she finally got some other reaction from me. "I honestly thought you wouldn't get beyond first base. *Maybe* second if you were really drunk."

"Well, I wasn't the slightest bit drunk," I say,

still not lifting my eyes from my laptop. I upload the spreadsheet and press send, relieved to be done with work for the week. Now I can concentrate on the oligopoly assignment for Monday. But instead of opening my assignments folder, I find myself browsing YouTube for mock job interview videos. They haven't done much for my interview skills so far, but I feel more competent just by watching them.

"What are you doing?" Jess exclaims the moment the video starts.

"Trying to pick up tips so I don't suck so badly at my next interview," I say, searching for a notepad so I can jot down anything the on-screen fake interviewee does that might come in handy.

She whistles. "I still can't believe you seriously want to work in investment banking. You do know you're selling your soul to the devil?"

I smirk. It's impressive how the (very true) rumors about the crazy working hours in banking have reached the ears of all the students, not only those studying Economics.

"I'm used to working hard," I say.

"You won't even have time to spend that ridiculous paycheck they'll give you. And anyway, having money doesn't mean your life will be perfect."

I agree, it doesn't. But having money helps. I

can take care of my parents.

"Can you—"

"Jess, if you don't let me concentrate, I'll be getting my paycheck from McDonald's. Or Wal-Mart."

The second the video stops, she says, "So how was the sex?"

I turn bright red. "Don't you have anywhere to be?" I mumble. "You said you want to take more shifts in the cafe this month."

"I took everyone's shifts for the weekend so I'm free today. Please tell me something. Anything. How was it?"

"Fantastic," I say without hesitation. There is no other way to describe it. Especially when I compare it to what Michael and I were calling sex.

I have been trying not to think of that night for the past week, because every time I do I drown in guilt and shame. Not because I regret it, quite the opposite. I'd do it again in a heartbeat, but I can't because James hasn't shown any signs that he's aware of my existence, despite asking for my number. I'm not looking for commitment, but I was hoping this would lead to several one-night stands. But not one. That's just cruel.

After introducing me to true passion and all of its wonders, robbing me of them shouldn't be legal.

I look up and find Jess staring at me with an ear-to-ear smile.

"Must be really fantastic if you have that expression just from thinking of it. So are you two now—"

"I haven't heard from him since. I think that makes us exactly nothing."

"Have *you* called him?"

"What?"

"I think the next Zuckerberg needs a reminder," she says, turning her tablet. I can only make out the title of the Forbes article, which is indeed "The Next Zuckerberg," and James's picture next to it. I refused to look up any info on him, thinking I'll forget the whole thing faster. "You do have his number, don't you?"

"Yeah, but—"

"So give him a call."

"Which place does this occupy on your dating advice list?" I ask sarcastically.

"You wouldn't be asking him on a date." She rolls her eyes then arches her eyebrows. "Booty call."

"No way." I grimace. "I have tons to do for Monday anyway," I say and start looking for the assignment on the Stanford intranet.

"Oh stop being such a good girl. It's your last semester. Have some fun. Anyway I'm sure Aidan will let you copy it from him if you smile nicely."

Aidan has the second highest GPA in my class after me. He also has zero social skills, which makes him turn a violent red and babble incoherently every time a girl pays attention to him. It wouldn't take much to convince him to let me copy the solutions.

I only realize what she's up to when I hear a distant dialing sound. I leap from my cross-legged position, sending my laptop crashing to the ground in the process, and launch myself over the table.

"Don't. Jess, I swear—"

It's futile. She holds my phone up in the air, too far away for me to grasp it. Jess is my best friend in the whole wide world, but sometimes—like now—I get the strange urge to throttle her. "Jessica Haydn, hand me that phone."

"Certainly," she says after a few excruciating seconds, and I know there can only be one reason for it.

He picked up.

"Hi. It's, Serena," I say, straightening up and struggling to even my breathing.

"Finally! I've meant to call you, but your number was incomplete."

"What?"

"Missing two digits."

I am *such* an idiot.

"So, to what do I owe the pleasure, Serena?"

The sound of my name in his mouth instantly brings back memories of all the other times he called my name.

"Umm," I look up at Jess, who mouths the word *plans* over and over. "I was wondering if you… already have plans for tonight?"

"What do you have in mind?" he says, sounding amused.

"Nothing special," I say quickly, feeling more embarrassed with every second.

"Then you can drop it?"

"Drop what?" I say confused and Jess slaps her forehead.

"The nothing special you had planned and join me." He sounds even more amused than before.

Jess gives a triumphant squeal. I'd do the same if I weren't on the phone.

"Where?"

"You really think I'll tell you?" he teases and I can feel his conceited smile forming at the other end. "Can you be ready in half an hour? I'll pick you up."

Jess desperately shakes her head, pointing to my hair and mimicking that she's applying lipstick.

I roll my eyes at her. "Sounds good."

"Perfect," he says and hangs up, leaving me

breathing heavier than when I answered, though for quite different reasons.

Half an hour later I'm waiting in the courtyard, wondering when exactly I lost my mind. Probably the same time I lost my decency.

I smile to myself. I'm so much better without them.

I check my outfit in my reflection at the front door. Jeans and a white top, a choice Jess vehemently criticized. She brought me an array of her shortest skirts, insisting that this is not the time to shy away from showing some leg. To me it just seemed like trying too hard.

The sound of a car roaring behind me causes something in my stomach to flutter violently. I turn around, expecting the familiar Rover and find a gray Porsche instead. The flutter in my stomach becomes almost painful as I open the door and slide into the car.

James looks even hotter than I remember, wearing a dark green polo and stylish Ray-Ban sunglasses. I'm glad I can't see his eyes, because that would make coherent thinking even more difficult.

"New week, new car?" I ask as he drives away.

He raises an eyebrow. "You thought I would arrive in a Range Rover with a driver? That is

Dad's car. And Peter is his driver."

"So where are we going?"

"You'll see," he says and the corner of his mouth lifts in his trademark smile. “I’m happy you called, Serena.”

“Really?”

“Yes. I was going a bit nutty when I realized the number was incomplete. Tried about thirty different combinations for the last two digits before giving up.”

Wow. Wow. Wow.

"I promise we'll have a lot of fun."

The hair on the nape of my neck stands on end at the word *fun.*

"So how come the next Zuckerberg," I say mockingly, "gets to leave his office on Friday at five o'clock?"

He chuckles. "If you also mention the TechCrunch article from last Monday, I'll seriously consider reporting you for stalking activity. And by the way, I hate that comparison."

"Yeah, it's really unfair. You're much hotter than he is," I say without thinking. My face instantly feels like it's on fire and I look away, burying myself in my seat.

"That's very sweet of you." I can't tell from the tone of his voice whether he's mocking me or not but don't dare turn and check for fear my cheeks are as red as they feel. "We pitched to the last investors for this round today. It went well so I let everyone take off and celebrate."

"How high is the investment round?" I say, sitting up straight.

"You just read the title of that article, didn't you?" he smirks.

Damn.

"Sort of," I admit jerkily. I make a mental note to check what exactly he's doing when I get home.

"Two hundred million."

"Impressive," I say. "What's your valuation?"

"Nine hundred million."

"Wow," I say, stunned.

"We're hiring, by the way."

"I'll consider putting you on my long application list," I joke.

"Why not?" he says seriously.

"Because what you do is far too risky for me. I've heard of enough entrepreneurs going bankrupt."

"True, but that's part of the beauty in this. The risk."

"I'm a corporate girl," I say, thinking that I'll prefer the security of a paycheck to reckless risk any day. Of course, I've yet to receive any kind of positive answer from any bank I've applied to, so I hope that paycheck won't just remain wishful thinking. I fist my palms tightly, hoping the usual anxiety over my future won't show up now.

"So where did you apply?" he asks.

"To every investment bank I could find."

He laughs softly. "I remember you saying you also take computer science classes along with economics. Not applying for a job in that area?"

I look at him, truly stunned that he remembers that, since I just mentioned it in passing when we first met at the bar. "Computer science is just my minor. And I'm not very fascinated by it."

"I see. So you really want to work in investment banking?"

"Yeah."

"Have you ever worked in investment banking before?"

"I did an internship at Merrill Lynch last summer," I say proudly.

"Christ, I did one at Goldman Sachs before my senior year. Most boring three months of my life."

"I liked it," I say briskly.

"Really?"

No, not *really*. But then again, what do I like? I've been having this dilemma ever since I started jotting down on a piece of paper names of banks to apply to back in October. Jess handed me a second piece of paper (with the title *What I Want to Do in My Life* written in pink tones with a little heart-shaped cardboard attached to it), insisting that I fill it with the things I love doing most. I looked up professional chocolate-tasting jobs for a few hours before giving up.

The *What I Want to Do in My Life* paper remains a blank page.

But the page with the list of banks I plan to apply to is anything but blank. It keeps growing every day. It was embarrassingly short in the beginning—I only looked at cities close to San Francisco, so Michael wouldn't have to commute to work once I got a job and we moved in together. Which I was sure was going to happen once I graduated. I almost snort at the thought now. Once he left me, I found out the world was much larger. New York and Washington made my list the night he broke up with me.

"What makes you so sure I'd be of any use to you?" I ask.

"Dean Kramer," he answers.

My jaw drops. "Who's the stalker now?" I ask in a strangled voice, but fact is, I'm elated that he talked with someone about me. Dean Kramer, no less.

"He called to ask me to give a talk next week and I casually told him we're looking for people. He wouldn't shut up about you."

I smile brightly, wondering what he's got in

store for today, but then I'm disappointed. The vast, perfectly cut fairways of the golf course lie on our left.

"You've got a really low standard for fun activities."

"We're not going golfing, Serena," he chuckles.

God, why does my name sound so hot coming from his mouth? Why does he have such an effect on me? He hasn't even said it in a flirty or alluring way.

He hasn't even kissed me today.

I turn to him, prepared to rectify this right away when he announces, "We're here." One second later we turn left down a narrow street, and the sight of two dozen small aircrafts in the distance momentarily distracts me.

I have flown three times before, but I have never used the Palo Alto Airport. It's small and only for private use.

"We're flying?" I ask, stunned, as he parks in front of the wire fence that marks the ending of the airport.

He turns the engine off and removes his glasses.

"Still not interesting enough for you?" he asks with a smile more conceited than ever, and gets out of the car. I hesitate for almost a minute before pushing the door open and stepping into the dry, evening air with an uneasy feeling.

"You don't look happy," James says, closing my door and looking at me with genuine concern.

"Not a fan of flying," I admit. "It makes me sick."

"You won't get sick, I promise." He wraps one arm around my waist and silences my protest with a kiss. Soft. Sweet. Short.

It's enough to awake the craving that overcame me at the party.

"I'm glad you called," he says in a low voice that tells me he shares my yearning.

"Glad enough to go somewhere else?" I murmur half-joking, half-serious.

He stares at me intently for a few seconds, then lets go of my waist with a dead-serious expression. "Was that a booty call?"

"What? No. I just—I mean, I'd rather not fly." When he still looks unconvinced I add, "When you said it will be fun I thought that—" I stop mid-sentence because he bursts out laughing and pulls me toward him again. My cheeks burn.

"I meant sex? You're adorable." Something flutters joyfully in my stomach. He places a soft kiss on my cheek and then slides away, biting my earlobe. "Don't worry, there'll be plenty of it later," he whispers in my ear.

"I would never have taken you for the booty call type," he jokes.

"Remind me to introduce you to Jess sometime," I mumble as he lets go of me.

"Let's go," he urges and we start walking toward the only door along the fence. "The others have been waiting for a while already."

"**O**h," I exclaim, hurrying after him. The thought that we wouldn't be alone never crossed my mind. As we slide between aircrafts, I wonder who exactly the others are.

My answer comes in an English accent. "You took your time, all right."

Parker appears in the doorway of the only plane with a ladder attached to it. Without his mask, the similarities between Parker and James are not so apparent anymore. Parker's cheekbones are more pronounced and his hair and eyebrows lighter; right now they're so arched they almost get lost in his hairline. I assume my unexpected presence is at fault for that. He recovers quickly, and smiles. "Lovely to see you again, Serena. Now, both of you get inside." He disappears from the doorway.

"James, I really don't think this is a good idea," I say, eying the small aircraft. It looks fancy and stylish, but I get grossly sick even on a Boeing 737. A tight knot forms in my throat. It can only get worse in this one.

"It's not as small as it looks," James says, looking at me amused.

"I—"

He puts his hand around my shoulders. "I'll find a solution if you get sick."

"I will get sick," I say but the reassurance in his tone made the knot in my throat loosen. I take one deep breath and start climbing the ladder.

He is right, the plane isn't that small. There are twice as many seats as I thought—six sleek leather chairs, arranged in three rows of two. All of their occupants wear an expression of stunned surprise, except Parker and the guy next to him, who's asleep, leaning on the window with his mouth hanging open. His shaved head reminds me of an egg.

"Everyone," James says, putting an arm over my shoulders, "I want you to meet Serena."

"Serena, you already know Parker. This is Thomas, Ralph—the one who's asleep—, Angela, Christie, and Natalie." My gaze freezes on the last face. Natalie is the lark. And she seems as happy to see me as I am to see her.

As I wave at everyone, I find myself inadvertently wondering if James was ever involved with Christie and Angela. They're both tall and attractive. Christie's got beautiful green eyes and blonde hair, and Angela resembles an angel more than anyone I've encountered in my life. I remind myself that it shouldn't matter if he did.

James gestures to the two seats on the row next to Christie and Natalie. I choose the window one and buckle my seatbelt the instant I sit down. James watches me chuckling. "Someone wake up Ralph," he says.

"God no, he's so much more fun when he's asleep," Christie says and everyone laughs, releasing some of the tension caused by my presence.

"Where are we going?" I ask, realizing I still have no idea.

"Nowhere, unless you count the clouds as a destination," someone says from the back. Thomas I think. "And that wouldn't be acceptable unless you're high already." Another round of laughter.

I stare at James confused. He wears an ear-to-ear grin that for the first time doesn't look conceited. "We're skydiving," he says just as the plane starts moving.

"What?" I ask blankly. "Who's we?"

The plane is now at the speed at which my stomach usually starts performing those somersaults that precede violent rounds of vomiting. The front wheels unhitch from the runway and I sink deep in my seat, closing my eyes. And my mouth, just in case.

"It will be fun," James calls to me.

"You're mental if you think I'll jump," I say and quickly shut my mouth again. I dig my nails in the leather, waiting for the somersaults and cramps to start.

They don't. Who knew that being scared out of your wits is the remedy to airsickness?

When the seat belt sign rings I finally open my eyes, and find James watching me amused.

"You need hours of training and practice and special equipment," I say, citing every possible reason that could convince him this is the worst idea ever. My desperation seems to have the opposite effect, because he's grinning even wider than before. "And you need guts," I add in a low voice.

James leans in, lifting my chin with his palm. "You have them," he says in an equally low tone, "you just need to let loose."

"Why aren't we ascending anymore?" the lark laments.

"We're only jumping from 7,000 feet today," James clarifies. “Serena is new to this.”

Natalie groans. "I wouldn't have bothered coming if I knew."

"I'll let you know next time," James says in a glacial tone, not looking away from me.

"So what do you say?" he inquires, his tone

warm and soft again.

"I have a choice?"

He stares at me intently, without one hint of a smile. "You always do."

And maybe because I can't bear disappointing him, or because I don't want to give the lark the satisfaction of witnessing my cowardly side, or because I truly lost my mind, I answer, "I'll do it."

His face breaks into a smile. "You'll love it." He unbuckles his seatbelt and gets up. "Let's get the equipment, Parker."

The equipment, as I find out five minutes later, consists of a heavy Supplex jumpsuit that covers my entire body, a helmet, and goggles. And a parachute, of course, but I don't get one because you truly need a lot of training to be able to steer it properly. I will jump with James.

"How do you feel?" Parker asks, setting up my helmet. James is in the cockpit, talking to the pilot.

"Like an Eskimo," I answer.

He grins. "It gets quite warm, doesn't it?"

"Hot, actually."

"Don't worry about anything, okay? James's been doing this for years. We all have."

"I'm not worrying," I say.

I should be terrified, but I'm not even scared. Of course it could just be that I'm so paralyzed by fear I can't tell anymore. But it can't be. I wouldn't be feeling this lightness in my chest if I were paralyzed. I don't know what it is, but it's not fear.

A piercing yelp at the back of the plane makes Parker and me jump.

"Damn it, Christie," Ralph bellows. He wipes his eyes, after Christie throws a glass of water in his face. "If you ever do that again—"

"If you'd actually wake up like any normal human being I wouldn't have to do it. Put on your suit, we're jumping in five minutes."

Ralph gets up grunting, and snatches his equipment from Christie's arms before she turns to join Angela and Natalie at the back of the plane, as they help each other. Predictably, Ralph's eyes enlarge to the size of oranges when he sees me and I open my mouth to introduce myself, but he turns away and starts putting on his jumpsuit without a word.

"I got this, Parker," I say, adjusting the straps on my shoulders. "Go and put your helmet on."

"All right." He strides over to his seat and I unclasp my necklace because both Thomas and Angela warned me at least twice to take off all jewelry.

Crap. The moon-shaped pendant slides off the necklace and lands on the floor with a thump, rolling under the seats. I crawl on all fours, peeking under the chairs and locate it a few seconds later, not far from Parker's foot.

I freeze in the act of making a grab for it when I hear Ralph saying in a low voice, "Who's the new chick?"

"James's girl," Parker replies.

"Christ, he's gonna start bringing them to our group activities?"

"Shut it," Parker hisses.

Ralph says something I don't understand. But I do catch Parker's angry reply. "It's his plane. He can bring whoever he wants."

I smuggle back the pendant without either of them seeing me and return to my seat, smiling. I should be mad, but I'm flattered instead. I'm the first woman he brought to the group.

"You look dashing," James says, reappearing from the cockpit.

"You're not so bad yourself," I say, but unlike him, I really mean it. Somehow, he manages to look hot even in the ridiculous suit.

"Come here." He stands behind me and sets up the belts and straps that connect us with sure hands as everyone comes to the front. "Serena and I will jump first," he announces and the lightness in my chest spreads to my stomach.

There's a metal bar just above the door that goes all the way to the front seats. James and I position ourselves next to the door and grab the bar, the rest lining up behind us.

"Ready?" he calls.

I barely nod when the door opens and James shoves me forward. In the blissful second between the first rush of cold air and my feet leaving the floor of the plane, I recognize what the lightness in my chest means: adrenaline.

There is nothing except the cold air filling my lungs… my mind… everything… in the free fall. My body is as light as a feather, as quick as a bullet. I hurtle down fast, fast, fast, the clouds appearing in a swirl around me, then disappearing again. A violent pull ends the incredible velocity and starts a smooth descent—James opened the parachute. I gasp involuntarily, as I take my first deep breath.

"You okay?" he screams in my ear.

"Never better," I scream back, my heart still racing so frantically I'm afraid it might jump out of my chest. A twinge of regret weasels itself in—I liked the speed. A lot. But its absence has perks, like being able to finally take in the beauty around me. It's breathtaking: the white, porous, unevenly shaped clouds floating around, the unending ocean and the red sun, preparing to sink in the blue waters in the distance, and even the mundane world below us—the highways and the golf club—looks almost perfect from here.

Parker, Thomas, and Ralph float around us, the girls higher. As we descend lower and lower, I find myself wishing we could go even slower.

We land faster than I'd hoped we would, in a rather large patch of sunburned grass right next to the airport. James undoes the connecting belts and straps almost immediately. The first few steps on the solid ground still feel like I'm floating.

"How was it?" James calls. He frees himself from the parachute and unzips his suit a little. We both throw down our helmets at the same time. The smile on his face is ecstatic.

"I loved it," I cry, unable to refrain myself from jumping up and down. "Can we go again?"

"Not today," he says, grinning widely. "It's really dangerous for you to try out new things. You always want more, don't you?"

I blush violently because I know he's not referring only to skydiving.

"Only if it's good," I answer and he bursts out laughing.

He grabs both my hands and pulls me into an embrace. "I was under the impression you found last Saturday more than good."

He entangles his fingers in my hair and pushes me against him for the first real kiss today. It's passionate, fierce, and almost desperate. It leaves me breathless and wanting more, cursing the suits and where we are.

"You're a wild little beast," he whispers, biting my lip.

Wild. Maybe.

Reckless. Yes.

That's how I behaved last Saturday and how I am behaving now. It's not the behavior itself that scares me. The fact that I chose to act this way scares me. I wanted to be reckless. As I look into his eyes, and feel his hot breath on my lips, every inch of my body tells me that I don't want to stop being reckless. He kisses me again.

"Damn. If all people would skydive, Pfizer would make no money on Viagra," Christie calls, and we stop.

We turn toward her, and all the others grouped around her, in various stages of removing their equipment—as if nothing happened.

"We voted earlier and *unanimously* decided we want to go to the Chinese restaurant downtown," Christie announces pompously.

"I'm with you if you want steak though, mate," Thomas says and Christie throws him a look that screams *traitor*.

"We won't be joining you." James puts an arm around my waist and kisses my temple. "I promised Serena there would be just the two of us the rest of the evening."

I flush so violently I think steam might come off my face any second. No one seems to share my embarrassment. Natalie rolls her eyes, and Thomas looks disappointed to have lost any chance of getting a steak tonight.

"Can we please go change?" Angela complains, her torso already half out of her suit.

The airport's restroom is minuscule, like the rest of the building, and not particularly suited for freshening up. But once out of my suit, I hurry and splash water on my face and neck at one of the three sinks, wondering why I hadn't thought of bringing anything more than a brush with me. At least I brought this with me, because my hair looks like I've been in a tornado. A few strokes later, I realize it will probably keep this look until I wash it. I sigh and stuff the brush back in my bag.

The door cracks open and a look in the mirror tells me Natalie has joined me. She doesn't acknowledge my presence and I follow suit, taking longer than necessary to search for the necklace in my bag. Out of the corner of my eye, I see her getting her entire makeup arsenal and carefully arranging everything on her sink.

"Don't fall in love with him," she says and I freeze in the act of pulling my necklace from the pocket I knew it was in all along.

"I'm sorry?" I put on my necklace with

trembling fingers.

"He doesn't *do* love."

My head snaps up. She's watching me in the mirror, a look of superiority obvious in every pore of her face.

"I'll keep that in mind," I say coldly.

"Oh, don't take it like that. I've known him for a long time. You barely met him. You're not even one of *us*." She pauses, watching me with large, expectant eyes, no doubt hoping I'll start a scene. I'm determined not to give her that satisfaction. "You seem like such a lovely girl, one who doesn't deserve to get hurt," she adds with disappointment, applying her mascara.

"Thanks for the advice," I say, fighting to keep my voice even.

"Why don't you keep the advice to yourself, Natalie?" Christie says from the doorway. I can't tell how long she's been there, but obviously long enough. "I'm pretty sure Serena can take care of herself."

I seize this moment to leave. Christie follows me and I don't intend to stop before reaching Angela and the guys, who are on the other side of the entrance door, chatting animatedly, when she says, "Don't pay attention to Natalie, okay? No one can spread venom better than her." She shakes her head.

"Was she lying?" I ask, stopping in my tracks.

Christie hesitates for a second before answering, "I wouldn't know from personal experience." She starts laughing at my sigh of relief, but resumes a serious demeanor when she adds, "From what I've heard, she wasn't lying. But this doesn't mean he can't change."

"Doesn't matter," I say quickly, wishing to cut this embarrassing conversation short. "It's just a bit of fun."

She raises an eyebrow.

"For both of us," I add and exit the small building, joining the group.

"I'm in the mood for a spontaneous trip to Malaysia," Ralph says. "Who's in?" He looks hopefully at the others.

James shakes his head. "Leave me out. I don't have time to join you."

He smiles when he sees me, and puts his arm over my shoulder.

"Neither will I," snaps Christie, jiggling her foot. "You could show some consideration for the others when planning such trips, Ralph. Not all of us are still living off our trust fund at twenty-eight."

Ah, yes. One of the things that will ensure I'll never be one of them. I finance my life at Stanford through scholarships and bookkeeping, not a trust fund. I take an involuntary look at Natalie, who just came out of the building. The look of superiority on her face hasn't faded one bit.

"That's your own fault," Ralph says. "I plan to enjoy the good life while it lasts."

He grabs Angela and Natalie by the waist. "What do you two dolls say about Malaysia next week?"

"Thomas, you in?" Angela asks.

"Of course."

"Parker?" the lark asks. Her lack of surprise at Ralph's words makes me wonder how often they go on such spontaneous trips around the world.

"He's part of the *responsible* group," Ralph says mockingly.

Parker chooses to ignore him and answers courteously, "Some other time, Natalie."

"Ah, I'll give Dylan and Simon a call. It'll be like a college reunion," Ralph screeches, kissing both Angela and Natalie on the cheek.

"So you all met at Stanford?" I ask.

"Minus Parker," Thomas retorts, a dreamy look starting to contour on his face. "Four insane years."

"I've known James and Parker since boarding school," Natalie says proudly.

James's arm on my shoulder turns rigid. His gaze, fixed on Natalie, is glacial. No one else reacts to her statement in any way, except Parker, who shoots Natalie a warning look.

"Serena and I will be going," James announces and after hurried goodbyes, in which Christie gives me a thumbs up, and Parker makes me promise that we'll meet up before he returns to London. Natalie ignores me as fully as I ignore her, listening to Ralph go on and on about Malaysia, and we head to the Porsche.

CHAPTER FIVE

"**Y**ou didn't have to do that," I say when we're both in the car. "I wouldn't have minded going out with them."

"I thought you'd be more comfortable if it's just the two of us," he says, driving out of the parking lot.

I stare at him, unsure what to make of this. Was the animosity between Natalie and me so obvious? Or did he anticipate all the trust fund and expensive trip talk would be awkward for me to listen to? Probably the latter. He, like Natalie, must be aware that I'm not one of them.

For a second I think about asking him what the deal with the boarding school was, but a glance at his still rigid fingers clasping the wheel tells me it isn't the best topic for conversation.

"So what now?" I ask playfully.

"Are you hungry?"

"Nope. Jess stuffed me with her famous paella earlier."

"Pity. I know a place in San Jose with the best chocolate fondue on the west coast."

"Chocolate fondue?" I squeak. "Really?" I blush as I realize he hasn't forgotten my little fondue story. Saturday night, he noticed a dark spot the size of a half dollar on my left thigh, a souvenir from a burn I got during one of my very few attempts at cooking: chocolate fondue. I read fourteen different recipes in preparation, and all I managed to come up with was a hard, grainy mess no one could look at, let alone eat. I kept to my truce with Jess ever since: she cooks, I clean.

Seeing what we were up to before and after this conversation, I'm amazed James remembered any of it.

"Should I take that as a yes?"

"You'd better." I grin.

We take the highway to San Jose, leaving behind the ocean and the sunset. I peek out the window, to see if I recognize anyone from the group behind the wheel of the cars we pass, but his speeding makes my task impossible. It also shortens our journey from the normal twenty minutes to twelve.

"Speed limits aren't your thing, huh?" I ask, clutching the edges of my seat, because he doesn't show any signs of slowing down even after we enter the city.

"Sorry," he says and hits the brakes so ferociously I'm positive I would've flown through the windshield if not for the seatbelt, which cuts deeply into my skin.

"Damn it, James," I cry.

He turns to me. "Are you all right?"

"Except for a near heart attack, yes."

"I'm sorry. I got lost in thoughts. I know I drive like a maniac."

"I'm fine," I interrupt, startled by the desperation in his gaze and voice. "We should get going. There's a line behind us."

We start again, this time at an almost embarrassingly slow speed.

"We don't have to let the slugs overcome us," I say.

He smirks at me, but there's something forced about it. Is he still thinking about Natalie's comment? The thought of asking him about it tempts me again, but I decide against it. I focus on the surroundings instead.

I was in San Jose once before with a group of enthusiastic, would-be entrepreneurs from my class, who wanted to attend a conference with the Valley's biggest venture capitalists—an inspiration in their entrepreneurial chase for the next big thing. I trailed along, because I rarely miss a free conference, and I must admit, between the speeches and the spectacular view from the top of the building we were in, the positive atmosphere was catchy. But I had read too many statistics on how few entrepreneurs succeed, how few ventures survive, let alone become as successful as James's, to get too excited. Many of my classmates plan to open their own businesses, or join a new venture in the Valley. I've never seriously considered anything besides banking.

We drive past the business district and its tall buildings, taking side street after side street, until we reach a park. James parks right next to the entrance.

"The restaurant is inside the park? Nice," I say as he turns off the engine.

I make a move to exit the car, but James interrupts, "Wait." He gets out of the car and comes over to my side, opening the door for me. Instead of saying thank you, I raise my eyebrows after I get out. He smiles widely. "I just thought I'd make a nice impression on our first official date."

A thousand butterflies flutter their wings simultaneously inside me, taking over my heart, leaving me breathless, "Oh."

He offers his arm and I take it clumsily, unsure what to make of the whole thing. I take a few deep breaths, trying to calm the wild drumming in my chest, hoping that my nervousness isn't visible in the dimly illuminated alley lined with palm trees. It's a lovely end of March evening.

The drumming reaches a new height when the restaurant comes into view, an elegant two-story cottage, with terraces on both levels, buzzing with people enjoying the warm evening.

"Welcome to L'Etoile," a pretty blonde with a tight bun and a heavy French accent greets us at the doorway. Her eyes rest on my jeans for a few seconds, then shift over to James's casual shirt. One closer look at the guests reveals that we're one suit and a chiffon gown too underdressed for this place.

James seems completely unperturbed by this. He unleashes the full force of his smile's charm on the poor woman a second later, when he says in a low voice, "James Cohen, I called for a reservation about two hours ago."

The woman's look of contempt instantly melts, the most ridiculous eyelash batting taking its place as she murmurs a weak "Follow me," before swirling around in her pumps and proceeding inside. Amazing, the effect he can have on women. I exchange a quick glance with James and both of us burst into less-than-discrete laughter. The woman trips over her own feet as she starts climbing a narrow spiral staircase. We don't head, as I expected, toward the terrace once we're on the second floor. The blonde leads us in the opposite direction to another door that opens to a balcony. When I step outside, my first thought is that the balcony is completely empty. Then I see the small table with two chairs. There are red candles in the middle of the table.

"That's our table," James says and I realize I've stopped walking.

"James, I… this is so… you didn't have to…"

Thankfully, he stops my incoherent babbling with a kiss. Soft and sweet in the beginning, until I feel the cold wall against my back, and James pressing himself against me, deepening the kiss with urgency. I can't suppress a moan when his hands find their way under my top, and James pulls away, gasping.

"Why don't we have that dessert before I change my mind?" he says in a low, raspy voice and turns around, taking my hand and leading me to the small table.

For once, I wouldn't mind skipping dessert. Even if it is chocolate.

The second we sit, a waiter appears out of nowhere, wearing an elegant white uniform and a polite, serious expression. I bite my lip, hoping he hasn't caught anything from the earlier scene. My entire face catches fire when I realize that even if he didn't see us, the blonde who led us here surely did. Why else would she have disappeared?

"What do you want to drink?" James asks me, already immersed in the menu.

"Whatever you're having."

The waiter bends to light up the candles, and as the small flames dance in front of my eyes, I can't help thinking of Michael and how we never had a candlelight dinner in our six years together.

James orders a French-sounding wine, chocolate fondue, and something else I don't catch, and the waiter disappears inside. To my astonishment, he returns almost immediately, holding a bottle of wine. He pours generously in both our glasses, then bows courteously and goes inside again. He doesn't reappear this time.

"A toast," James says, holding up his glass.

Our glasses meet in a sweet cling. "To this evening," he says, staring at me intently above the candles and I know he's expecting me to say something, but between the candles and the wine and the kiss I don't know what I could say that would do justice to all the feelings overwhelming me, without sounding like a complete idiot. So I sink my lips into the red liquid without one word.

I grimace a little.

"You don't like it? We can order another one."

"It's fine," I say quickly. "I just don't drink wine very often."

"I see," he chuckles, "only tequila."

I blush furiously. "No, that was a one-time thing because—"

"You wanted to hook up with someone and didn't have the courage?"

"Precisely," I say, keeping my eyes firmly on my plate.

His chuckle turns into full laughter. "In case you were wondering, it worked very well. You looked like you wanted nothing better than to spend the night with me… not exactly talking."

My head shoots up. "Why didn't you ask me to leave with you?"

"I don't usually take advantage of women." He puts his glass on the table, not taking his eyes off me.

"I wasn't *that* drunk," I say.

"No, you were angry and hurt. That's even worse."

I stare at him stunned. Of all inappropriate things I said that night, I don't remember ever mentioning—heck, not even hinting at—Michael.

How could he tell?

"I didn't want you to do something you might regret later. I honestly never thought you'd show up at my parents' house," he says, shaking his head as if the thought still surprises him. "But I'm glad you did."

"I'm glad too," I say.

"You are?" he asks, his expression unreadable.

"Why would I have called you today if I wasn't?"

"I think we already established the reason for your call," he laughs softly and I'm sure my face is as scarlet as the candles before me.

Two waiters appear on our balcony, each carrying a large tray. I frown as they start unloading.

A bowl of strawberries in front of me, a cup with three scoops of ice cream and a lot of whipped cream in front of James, and a small fondue burner in the middle. I can't help clapping my hands as he puts the fondue over the burner. Hot, liquid chocolate, waiting for me to devour. One strawberry at a time.

"What do you have?" I ask.

"Walnut, caramel and straciatella," James says, already taking a spoonful.

I stick the small fork in a strawberry and dip into the liquid chocolate.

"Oh my God," I say, "this is delicious. Aren't you going to eat anything?"

He shakes his head, taking another spoonful of ice cream. "Not a big fan of chocolate."

"So this is all for me?"

"By all means. We can order more if you want."

"No please, don't tempt me like this."

"So, tell me more about you, Serena."

"I'm a simple girl. I take classes, and I work to finance my studies."

"Your parents are in the UK?"

"Yes. And once I get a decent job, I plan to take care of them."

He smiles. "You're a lovely girl."

Two glasses of wine and all the strawberries later, I truly mean it when I declare "This is the best evening ever."

"It's not difficult to make you happy, is it?" James asks.

"Not if there's chocolate involved," I say, scooping the last drops of chocolate with his spoon. "Is your office far from here?"

"You can see it over there actually," he says, pointing to a spot over the trees.

"I don't see anything." I sway a little as I get up from my chair, and James hurries to steady me.

"Who gets wasted from two glasses of wine?" he says, amused.

"I am not wasted," I say. "I just have balance problems."

"Okay," he says, grabbing me by the waist with

one arm, and taking my right hand with the other, pointing up. "There."

And now I do see it. The skyscraper. The top of it, at least.

"Which floor is your office?"

Instead of an answer I get a kiss on my neck. And then another one. I dig my fingers in his hair and turn my head, desperately searching his lips. I find them at the same time his hands slide under my top. I don't know if it's the wine or the chocolate, or my desperate need for him finally, but I don't make any move to stop him as his hands go higher and higher, touching my breasts, my nipples. I don't want him to stop. I want him to touch me. All of me. Right here. Right now. He bites my lip and I moan deeply in his mouth.

It's only when one of his hands slides down and unzips my jeans that I come to my senses.

"Not here," I whisper, and for a frozen second, neither of us moves.

Then he grabs my hand. "Fuck, Serena. Let's go."

I sit as far from James as possible in the cab, so the cabbie can keep his eyes only on the road. James said he'll have someone bring his car to his building, because he had too much to drink tonight. Neither of us utters one word the entire trip. I jump out as soon as the cab stops in front of the high-rise. James pays the driver and joins me a few seconds later. He takes my hand and leads me inside the luxurious building. I wish he'd offer me his arm instead because I still don't feel like I could walk straight.

"Good evening, Mr. Cohen," the tall, middle-aged concierge greets us.

"Daniel." James nods, without one look in his direction.

Our shoes clink loudly on the white marble and it vaguely occurs to me that Daniel must suspect why we're in such a hurry. But any thoughts of shame vanish from my mind when the metal doors of four elevators come into view. In just a few seconds James and I will be alone. Yet when the doors open, my stomach drops in disappointment.

The elevator is not empty. An elderly couple, probably coming from the garage, chat lively over the brochure the husband is holding. They fall silent when we enter, and smile politely. James presses the button to the top floor and the elevator swooshes up with nauseating speed. I lean on the back mirror to steady myself, keeping my eyes firmly away from James. He doesn't grant me the same mercy. I feel his gaze over me, piercing me.

The following minutes pass by as if in a dream.

Our journey lasts for three more floors, then we step out and James takes a painfully long time to unlock his door.

Finally there's only passion: his lips on my neck, his hands on my bare thighs, and my unskilled attempts at getting rid of his shirt, his jeans, and everything else that stands between his skin and me. We're both completely naked when he lifts me in his arms.

"The bedroom's not that far away," he teases in response to my surprised yelp. I rest my head on his shoulder as he carries me through the darkness, moving my fingers playfully over his chest. He doesn't put me down on the bed, but in front of it, standing with my back to him. I make a move to turn around, but his hands on my hips keep me firmly in place. "I want you like this," he orders.

"It's not fair, I can't touch you," I whisper, my hands desperately seeking his skin.

He bends me down, and I put my palms on the bed. He runs a finger down my spine, sending waves of cold shivers through me. And then he slams against me. Hard. One desperate moan after another escapes my lips as he thrusts again and again, harder and harder until I'm afraid my knees will give in.

"James, wait," I gasp, and he lifts me with one arm, propping my knees on the bed without me having to ask for it. I straighten up, flattening my back against him, seeking his lips.

"Do you want me to touch you?" he demands in a raspy, low tone as his thrusts become more brutal, his breaths more convulsive.

"Yes," I beg him. "Yes, please."

"Show me how much you want it," he commands. I take his hand from my hip and place it on my damp sex, more aware of my body than ever. And then he starts moving his blessed fingers around in little circles, my nails digging deep in his thigh as I climax. My entire body shakes when he calls my name.

CHAPTER SIX

He helps me lie on the bed, and I almost fall asleep. Sometime later, a burst of laughter awakes me from my drowsy state. I open my eyes, immediately regretting it. Light. The source must be somewhere on the bedside table on the other side of the bed, where James lies, visibly less disheveled than me. And amused.

"What's so funny?" I ask weakly, wondering if I did something wrong earlier.

"This is absolutely the last time I'm going out in public with you when all I want is to make love to you. I've never lost my head like this in public, except at some frat parties, but they don't count."

There are several things about his sentence that make my stomach flip. First, the lovemaking thing. Surely only two people in a relationship talk about lovemaking. It's sex for the rest of us, isn't it?

Then there's the never before thing. Of all the hotties he's been with, can there really be a never before for him?

He kisses my forehead and gets up, announcing, "I need a shower. If you want something to wear, take anything from the closet. But I wouldn't mind seeing you run around naked." He winks and slips into the bathroom.

I sit up on an elbow and, for the first time, take in the room. Everything from the white leather bed to the satin sheets covering me and the sleek, gray carpet on the floor reminds me of those storefronts for home decor.

The masterpiece, though, is the glass wall directly opposite the bed, through which the entire city is visible. I get up and walk to the window, admiring the dazzling lights outside.

It's only when I get goose bumps all over my body that I realize I really do need something to wear. His closet is three times the size of mine, and I begin to randomly open doors, until I find the one I want, with towels and bathrobes. I start taking one of the bathrobes off the hanger, when I notice the shelf above has five folded velvet robes, similar to what Dani was wearing when I first met her, only more masculine. I rise on my toes and reach for the black velvet, but the shelf is so high I can barely touch the soft fabric. I pull at it as best as I can and next thing I know, all five robes land on my head and then drop to the floor with a thump.

I sigh and bend to pick them, when I notice a picture in between the black and gray velvet. James is in it. A much younger James, probably no more than eighteen years old. Next to him is a beautiful girl. Chocolate brown curls frame her perfect face and her large, round blue eyes look at James adoringly.

Two words are written in careful handwriting on the back of the photo. *Always, Lara.* I stare at them for a few seconds, then put the photo and four of the robes back on the shelf as best I can. I don't want him to think I'm snooping.

Just in time too, because James opens the door of the bathroom, declaring proudly, "I'm a completely new person."

"I need to become one, too, or your robe will pay the price for my laziness," I say, attempting to get past him—he's blocking the doorway to the bathroom.

He grabs me by the waist and gives me a quick kiss, then moves out of my way.

"I still think you shouldn't be wearing that," I hear him say before I close the door.

While I shower, I wonder about Lara. I suppose she was his girlfriend back when they were young.

I wonder if she's the reason behind James's disdain for his school years.

Why is he keeping her photo? Nostalgia? *It's none of my business.* We all have pasts, and I have no right to be jealous.

When I get out of the shower, James is nowhere to be found. I wrap the oversized robe tightly around me and head out of the bedroom, guessing my way through the penthouse. I find him in the living room, wearing shorts and a black T-shirt, staring outside through yet another glass wall, holding a glass of orange juice. He's talking on the phone.

"No, if it's in the garage in the morning it's fine. I don't need it now. Good evening to you too, Daniel."

"I always thought being an entrepreneur was all about ramen noodles and living in shared apartments."

He looks up at me and smirks. "It is in the beginning. If it's still like that after a few years, you don't know what you're doing."

"I'm sure you avoided that dreadful beginning, no?" I ask sardonically. "Isn't that the purpose of a trust fund?"

"Judgmental much?" He raises an eyebrow, but doesn't seem upset in the slightest.

"I'm just being realistic."

He stares at me intently for a few seconds, then empties his glass and says, "I busted my entire trust fund in college."

My jaw drops. "Are you serious?"

"My father was even less impressed than you are," he says with a wink.

"I bet. How on earth did you manage that?"

"I was something of an expert at spending exorbitant amounts of money. Luckily, running out of them taught me quickly how to make money, too. I sold my first company after two years." He raises his empty glass. "Something to drink?"

"Orange juice is fine," I say, still stunned.

We move to the kitchen, which is separated from the living room by a glass wall, and looks like it's never been used, with the exception of the fridge. When he opens it, I have a vision of what my own fridge would look like if I weren't living with Jess—full of unhealthy drinks and takeout boxes.

"So where did you get the initial investment?"

James shoves a glass of orange juice toward me. "Parker and Natalie were my first investors. They both own stocks in the company I have now too."

"Damn. Just when I was about to start admiring you for making it on your own," I tease, taking another sip of juice and hoping that my sudden apprehension isn't visible.

He lowers his glass, revealing his trademark smile, more conceited than ever. Before I realize what's going on, his arms are around my waist, his lips whispering in my ear, "I've got other means of impressing you."

My body makes no secret of it—the skin on my entire body burns, and my hips press against his without me ever ordering them to do so.

I expect him to run his fingers up the inside of my thighs, like he always does when he wants me. Instead, he lets go of me and gestures for me to follow him.

"Come on, there's something I want to show you."

"For your sake, I hope it's another bedroom."

"You never get enough, do you?" He chuckles and takes my hand, dragging me through the penthouse. We pass door after door, and stop in front of the only entry I'm sure doesn't lead to a bedroom—a sliding door.

"Close your eyes."

"I'd rather not," I say nervously.

"Trust me," he says in a playful voice. "You'll like this more than the bedroom. In fact, you'll like it so much I'm afraid I'll have some convincing to do to get you out of there again."

"Okay, now I trust you even less," I stutter, but

close my eyes.

The unmistakable sound of the door sliding open follows and then he half-guides, half-pushes me forward a few feet.

"Open your eyes."

"No way," I cry.

Five rows of comfortable, red armchairs complete with support for plastic cups unravel before me. On the wall in front of them is a huge screen.

"Is this a real screening room?" I ask in a strangled voice.

"Yes it is," he brags. "Want to see the movie collection?"

"This really is the best evening ever," I say as he opens the computer resting on a small table behind the last row of chairs.

Three minutes later, I'm immersed in the movie database, hardly believing my eyes.

"You look like you've stumbled upon a gold mine," James says.

"I can't believe there's a bigger movie freak than me," I say. "Do you have every movie ever made in here?"

"That's the goal," he retorts.

"Damn, and I was so proud of my DVD collection," I say.

"How many do you have?"

"313. 312 actually, because I loaned *Fight Club* to the French exchange student that was living next door last year, and she never bothered to return it," I say angrily. "Oh my God, you've got *The Lion King*."

"Of all movies, you're impressed with *The Lion King*?"

"Mufasa dying gets to me every time," I say.

"Me too," he admits. "So what do you want to watch?"

"I get to choose what we watch?" I say, restraining myself as much as possible from clapping my hands, because that would be even more childish than swooning at the sight of *The Lion King.*

"Of course you get to choose. I guess the bedroom lost the battle already," he says, wrapping his arms around me.

"Umm, just for a little while, I promise." I struggle to keep my voice even as he bites my earlobe softly. "I love your penthouse," I murmur.

"You can come here anytime," he whispers in a raspy voice.

His invitation has the unexpected effect of turning my stomach to ice. With a pang, I realize why. There can be only one reason why he made the invitation so easily. It's one he often extends. To old lovers, like Natalie, and to almost strangers, like me. What a bitter thought… Natalie in his arms.

"Let's see if I find a movie I've never heard of," I say, scrolling down the endless list of movies. I have heard of all of them. I've seen most of them once. Some even twice. "How did you decide to have a screening room?"

"I love movies. I dare say I love them as much as you do. Dani is also a fan, and she comes here on weekends sometimes."

His voice is full of love as he speaks about his sister.

"You're close to Dani?"

"I love her more than anyone on this planet, and I like spending time with her. Do you have siblings?"

I debate changing the topic, because thinking about Kate makes me sad, but for some reason, talking to James feels natural.

"I had a sister. She died nine years ago from an overdose."

"I'm sorry." James wraps his arms around me. "Do you want to talk about it?"

"It's a sad topic."

"I can see that it still hurts you. But talking can help."

Before I know it, words start pouring out of my mouth. Words I have never uttered before, not even to myself, let alone to another living soul. They speak of pain and guilt, and about missing her every single day.

It's a while before I notice we're sitting on the floor, James leaning against the wall and me, curled up in his arms, resting my head on his chest. There's something calming about listening to his heartbeats, echoing so clearly in the silence between us.

“Oh, James. Now I’ve ruined the mood.”

“No, you didn’t.”

"It happened so long ago, and I never talk about it…"

"Doesn't matter when it happened," he says softly. "The pain never really goes away. You just learn to survive with it."

My heart skips a beat. He's the first person to tell me this. I’ve suspected it for a long time, even though everyone insists that time heals everything.

"If I'd looked more closely after her," I whisper. He pulls me closer to him, caressing my cheeks with the back of his fingers.

"Then maybe she would have lived a day, a month, a year longer. But how much longer, Serena? You can't be someone's guardian angel forever," he says firmly.

Guardian angel… The words bring back a very old memory. I was ten when Kate's problems began. I didn't understand what was going on, I just knew that my sister wasn't behaving like my sister anymore. So I used to pray every night after my mother tucked me in bed, asking my guardian angel to leave me and go at Kate's side, because her angel seemed to be a tad overwhelmed. When it became clear to me that either my guardian angel wasn't listening to me, or she had listened to me but she too was overwhelmed, I decided to take the matter in my own hands. Some help I turned out to be.

"Don't blame yourself for something that was out of your control. There was no other end to the path she'd taken."

"Maybe," I say, "but it didn't have to end that day."

"Any other day would've hurt you just as much. Do you have nightmares?"

I shudder in his arms. How can he know?

"Sometimes," I admit, "but not very often."

"You're a remarkable person," James says, and the suppressed tension in his voice sends cold jitters down my back. "To carry all that pain and not lose yourself on the way."

"I didn't really have a choice."

He gives a humorless laugh. "There's always a choice, Serena. And trust me, most people don't choose your way."

"What do most people choose?" I raise my head slightly, searching for his eyes, but he's looking in the opposite direction. Something tells me the real question is, *What did you choose?*

It finally dawns on me why he can see the pain, why he knows about the nightmares. He, too, must have lost someone. Was it Lara?

I run a finger along his neck and he turns toward me, gazing at me with kind yet determined eyes. I know he won't tell me anything. Not tonight. Another time, if I'm lucky, I'll hear his story. I will learn about his pain, and maybe I will be able to soothe his wounds the way he soothed mine.

Maybe, just maybe then he'll forget her.

"So, what's it gonna be?" I ask playfully. "*The Lion King*? Or do you prefer *The Godfather*?"

"Your wish is my command," he answers in an equally playful tone, planting gentle kisses on my neck, then gets up, pulling me after him. This even is surprising on so many levels. James is surprising. I expected us to have some fun, but I wasn't expecting for us to bond. He isn't just a fun, rich guy. He is someone who knows loss, and loves his sister, and both things endear him to me.

Oh, Serena, don't get your hopes up.

This is nothing serious. He was upfront with me from the start. I'm the first woman he took to meet his friends, though. I'm giddy at the thought, and despite everything, I can't help but hoping that maybe this will evolve into more than a little fun.

CHAPTER SEVEN

I spend the entire weekend with James, only returning to my apartment on Monday morning. We didn't make plans aside from a casual *I'll call you*, and by Wednesday, I find that I miss him, even though we spoke on the phone every day.

I'm with Jess, in front of the Stanford Memorial Auditorium. The longer I stand on the burning pavement, the more tempted I am to jump in the fountain. The fact that almost one thousand students will witness my rule breaking doesn't seem reason enough not to do it…The fine I'd get for doing it does, though. The rivulets of sweat forming on my back might make even the fine seem insignificant in a few minutes.

"I still don't get why you dragged me to this conference. I don't care about the economic downturn or whatever crap they always talk about," Jess complains, holding her notebook on the side of her face, in a poor attempt to block the blinding sun.

"It's not about the downturn. And listening to some smart people won't hurt you," I say, still eying the fountain. I take a sip from my ice-cold smoothie, the only thing standing between me and a jump in the fountain.

"Smart is relative. I should be preparing for my phone interview tomorrow."

Jess's job search has been going so much better than mine. She credits it to her vision board, a complex extension of her own pink *What I Want to Do in My Life* paper. I credit it to her mind-blowing confidence.

"You had enough time this morning. You need a change of scenery."

The crowd starts moving inside slowly, and Jess jiggles her foot impatiently.

"Let me finish this," I say, sipping the last remains of the smoothie.

"Tell James you like kiwi smoothies," she says with a grin. "Maybe he'll take you to a kiwi plantation or something."

I grin back. After painfully detailed questioning of my weekend, Jess decided that James is the perfect boyfriend. She blatantly ignored me when I pointed out that he made it crystal clear he isn't my boyfriend.

"Jess, are you jealous?" I tease.

"Obviously. How can this guy be real? He introduced you to his friends, took you out to a candlelight dinner, and finds your movie obsession cute."

"He's a movie freak too."

"I've lied to myself my whole life that guys like him don't exist," Jess says, as if she hasn't heard me, "but I keep running into assholes who can't introduce me to their friends after six months of dating." Her grin fades into a sad smile.

I know exactly who she means: Ethan, the guy she proclaimed was the love of her life until three months ago, when she abruptly dumped him. But she all but forbade me to ever talk about him.

"Let's go inside," I murmur. "Oh shoot—turn around," I command and swirl around, grabbing Jess by the shoulder.

"Ouch. What was that for?" she complains.

"Abby just passed by. I told her I missed the last two Saturday volleyball games because I had chickenpox."

Jess bursts out laughing. "You're an awful liar."

"She is." I raise my gaze and find James standing a few feet away from us, in front of the fountain. He's dressed in a suit, and my heartbeats become lightning-fast. I curse my wardrobe choice—an above-the-knee gray cotton dress with short sleeves. I thought it made me look like a smart, would-be professional when I chose it. I feel like a desperate schoolgirl now.

Jess steps forward. "I'm Jessica Haydn," she says, almost out of breath.

"James. Nice to finally meet you." He kisses Jess on both cheeks then turns his attention to me. "You look perfect for someone who was supposed to be down with chickenpox for two weeks," he muses.

"I had to come up with something," I mumble, staring at my feet.

"Are you joining us in the auditorium, James? Getting bored to death by lousy speeches is much less painful when in good company," Jess says.

"I'm actually here to deliver a speech." He smirks at her.

"I'll make sure not to fall asleep during yours, then." She winks. “I'll be eternally grateful if you crack a joke or two. You're twenty-eight, which makes you a good fifteen years younger than all the other speakers, so I'm putting all my trust in you.” Jess will never cease to amaze me. Is there anything that could ever throw her off, or shake that fantastic confidence of hers even a bit?

"You were not on the speaker list," I say to James. "I checked it twice."

"I promised Dean Kramer that I'd show up spontaneously if I had time."

"I'll wait for you inside, Serena. Nice meeting you, James," Jess dismisses herself, and I wonder if it's finally a sign of embarrassment or she just wants to give us some space.

"Let's go somewhere in the shade," he says, undoing the top button of his shirt.

We stop under the valley oak next to the auditorium and I lean against the rough bark.

"We should go inside. The first speech will start in a few minutes," I say.

"I didn't come out here for the speech," James says, his lip curling into a delicious smile. He leans so close I can feel his warm, sweet breath on me. "I saw you and wanted to see you."

My heart skips a beat. How can I not melt at such words?

He leans in even closer, and I expect him to kiss me, but he stops just one inch short of my lips. It takes me a second to realize he's asking for my permission. I close the distance with a soft kiss, then pull back quickly.

He looks at me questioningly.

"Someone can see us," I murmur.

"You weren't that concerned when we landed on Friday."

"That was different."

For a few seconds neither of us says anything, then he lifts my chin with his right hand. "Is everything all right?"

"Sure. I just... would feel weird if anyone saw us. You being a speaker and all."

He lets go of my chin, and takes a step back, looking at me. "You look hot in this dress."

"Don't mock me."

"I'm serious. Makes me even sorrier that I have to go in for that speech. What are you doing tonight? I'm leaving for a short business trip tomorrow, and I'd like to spend this evening with you."

"I can't. I have plans."

"Sending another batch of CVs? I thought you said you almost exhausted your list of banks."

"I actually added a few dozen more to the list last night."

He grins. "Because 112 applications are not enough?"

"I'm doing something else tonight," I say, avoiding his gaze.

"What?" He's suddenly inches away from me, clutching my arms in his hands.

"It's nothing, just... a thing I do sometimes." Sometimes meaning every Wednesday.

"Which is?" His grip on my arms tightens. I raise my eyebrows and he removes his hands.

"Are you seeing someone?" he asks in a strained voice.

"I never took you for the jealous type," I challenge.

He flinches visibly, his eyes widening. "I'm sorry."

"For the record, I'm not seeing anyone but you. I'm dressing up as a clown for a few hours in a show at the local hospital for kids with leukemia."

His glower melts into a surprised smile. "That's very admirable of you," he says and kisses my forehead.

"I started doing this after…you know."

"It helps you?"

"Sort of. It helps them a lot which… helps me."

A loud beep makes us both jump. It comes from inside—the sign that the first speech has begun.

He kisses my forehead again and murmurs, "Call me after you finish." Then his lips move to my ear and he says playfully, "I missed your coffee."

I give a nervous giggle. I woke up with the firm determination that we both needed a strong dose of caffeine on Sunday morning, after only having had about four hours of sleep the whole weekend. So I left a sleeping James and went to the nearest Starbucks, but instead of buying two cups of steaming hot liquid, I returned with a bag of ground coffee. What followed reminded me why I never do things spontaneously. Especially things I suck at. James woke up to the disgusting smell of burnt coffee and a filthy stove. Yet for all the warning signs, he still insisted on tasting my coffee. I never saw anyone spit anything with such desperation.

"One kiss before we go in?" he whispers, trailing his lips from my ear down the base of my neck.

CHAPTER EIGHT

"**P**lease let me do this," Jess pleads for the fifth time next morning.

"No, I want to do it," I say, keeping my eyes on the kettle. I didn't call James after I finished last night, because I stayed at the hospital much longer than I intended. After the show was over, Maya, one of the girls in the leukemia ward asked me to read her favorite bedtime story so she could fall asleep. How could I say no to a teary-eyed six-year-old?

"Are you sure he's even up at this hour?" Jess asks, hovering around like a drunken bee. She's normally asleep at this hour, but today she woke up early to prepare for her phone interview at nine. She froze in place when she spotted me in front of the stove.

"He said he's always up by six on weekdays and leaves for his office at seven."

"And you decided to wish him good morning by poisoning him?"

"No, I decided to do something nice for him."

Twenty minutes later, I park Jess's Prius in front of James's luxurious building, and grab the two plastic cups with trembling hands. They're still warm. And I know the coffee in them is decent enough because Jess gave me her full approval after testing it. She even poured a cup for herself.

I greet Daniel while I practically jog to the elevators, armed with the two coffee cups and a strange sense of bliss. I'm not sure exactly what brings it. Perhaps the fact that I'm wearing my favorite light blue dress or that I had my first culinary success. Oh, who am I kidding? Nothing except the thought of James's kisses can make my entire body tingle this way.

I press the bell with my elbow and wait patiently, afraid my heart will literally burst out of my chest when the door opens. But when it does open, it's not James who looks back at me. It's Parker. A *very* messed-up Parker. I do my best not to recoil at the sight of his bloodshot eyes.

"Serena," he says, looking even more stunned than when he saw me at the airport. "Hi, how—oh, you brought coffee?"

"I didn't know you'd be here, or I would have brought more," I say, trying to withhold a laugh.

"You know what, take mine. You look like you need it more than me. Is James's hangover as bad as yours?" He doesn't take the cup.

"James, no... He didn't drink that much... I mean..." he stutters.

"Can we continue the conversation inside?" I ask and push him from the doorway. I was expecting the living room to look as disheveled as Parker, but except for a wrecked blanket on the couch, indicating where he spent the night, everything looks as neat as it did when I was last here.

"James is in his room?"

"Yeah... but now is not a good time, Serena. Maybe you should leave and I'll tell James to call you later." There's no stutter in his voice anymore, and an uneasy feeling is starting to form inside me.

"Why?" I raise my head, trying to look in his eyes for the first time, but now he avoids mine. "Parker?"

"Parker, are you up?" James calls from a room, then joins us.

He looks at me in surprise, and opens his mouth, but before he can utter one word, Natalie walks in the room too. Her hair is wild and she wears an overlarge, manly T-shirt. Everything inside me clenches, and my eyes begin to sting. I was such a fool. *Such a fool.*

She looks at me with a smirk. I want to wipe it off her face.

“Good morning, Serena.”

"James, you don't mind if I join you in the office a bit later?" Parker says, putting one arm on my shoulders. "I promised breakfast."

"Don't be a prick, James," Natalie says when James doesn't answer. "Let the two of them go." When he still doesn't answer, she raises her eyebrows and adds, "I'm taking a shower," then disappears from the living room.

"Can you give us a moment, Parker?" His voice carves raw wounds inside me.

"That's not necessary," I say, finally lowering my arms from their twisted position at my back. James's gaze freezes on the coffee cups. "No, Parker—" I plead.

"You two need to talk, Serena," he says firmly and then walks out the front door.

"I didn't know you were coming," James says, still staring at the coffee cups.

"That's obvious," I answer sardonically. "I wanted to surprise you. But you beat me to it."

"I—"

"No, you know what? Don't say anything. I'm going to leave now and for the sake of my own sanity, pretend I never met you."

"You want to stop seeing me?" he says, shell-shock contouring on every pore of his face.

"No. I want to stick around and find a new woman in your bed every morning." I don't know when my pain transformed into anger, but I welcome the change. Being angry is so much better than being in pain. "Seeing you with other women..." I pause to find the word that would sound least dramatic, "...bothers me." I make a go for the door but he puts an arm around my waist.

"Serena—"

"You didn't seem too happy yesterday when you thought I was going out with someone," I say angrily.

"Serena, stop and listen to me. I didn't sleep with Natalie."

Everything stills inside me. I draw a deep breath.

"She's wearing your t-shirt."

"She must have found it in the guest room."

God, I want to believe him.

"What is she doing here?"

"Parker and I worked late last night, then went to have drinks. She joined us. She got very drunk. I couldn't just send her home. Nothing happened, Serena. Nothing."

I swallow, looking away. "She likes you. At your parents' party, she hinted that she likes you. And at the airport, she warned me off."

His jaw ticks. “She warned you off? I’ll talk to her. About the other thing…it’s true. She does want something from me. But I don’t want anything from her, do you understand? I just didn’t think it was safe to put her in a cab and send her on her way. Please say something. Say you believe me.”

“I do. I just…My ex cheated on me, and seeing her like this threw me off. And I have to go. I don’t feel comfortable being here just now.”

“I understand. I can clear my schedule and take you somewhere where we can talk.”

I shake my head. “No, I just came by to drop the coffees. Don’t cancel your trip.”

“I’ll see you when I return?” he asks with urgency.

I nod, but as I hear the door to the bathroom open, I whisper, “I really want to go now.”

I put both coffee cups on the table, and hurry out the door.

Parker unhitches himself from the wall when he sees me, walking with me to the elevator.

"I meant what I said about that breakfast," he says as we both step in the elevator.

“I don’t have time. I just wanted to drop by with coffee, see him for a bit before he left on his trip.”

"Quick breakfast? There is a nice coffee shop one block away."

I sigh, giving in. I am hungry after all.

Ten minutes later, we're sitting in a cozy coffee shop with sandwiches and coffee.

"You and James sorted everything out? You still look worried."

"He…he says she slept in the guest room, that nothing happened."

"It's true."

"Why did you insist I leave when I arrived?"

"Because I didn't think seeing Natalie would do you any good."

I bite into my sandwich, trying to make sense of this unease I'm feeling.

"She fits well in his world," I find myself saying.

Parker smiles kindly. "I believe James likes you specifically because you're different. I know finding Natalie there looked bad, but if he says nothing happened, then nothing happened. James doesn't lie."

I fiddle with my fingers, sipping from the coffee. "This isn't about him lying…It's more to do with a bad past experience I had. I have trust issues, I guess. I didn't even realize it until this morning."

Parker's expression grows sad. "Ah, I

understand. He admires you."

"He does?"

"Yes. He speaks very highly of you. In fact, I haven't heard him speak so much about someone he went out with before."

"Can I ask you something? Who is or was Lara?"

Parker presses his lips together. "He told you about her?"

"No, but I…would it help me understand him more if I knew about her?"

"I think so, but that's his story to tell. All I can say is that they dated in high school, and she died on our graduation day. It was a very sad affair. But I don't feel comfortable telling you more."

"And you shouldn't. You're right. This should be coming from James. But thank you for sharing this with me, for taking me to breakfast."

We make small talk as we finish our sandwiches and coffee, and my mind is racing, thinking about James's past and his hesitations, as well as my own.

***

When I return to the apartment, I find Jess on the phone, pacing like mad between the couch and the kitchen, speaking in a very formal tone. Her interview, of course. Jess stops dead in her tracks at the sight of me and raises her shoulders questioningly. I shake my head and walk directly to my room, where I finally find silence.

I pace, trying to understand what's wrong with me. Why do I feel so jittery? *Nothing* happened with Natalie. I guess what bothers me is that I jumped to conclusions so fast. Michael's betrayal did a number on me. What also bothers me is that I was so hurt at the mere idea that James had cheated. I wasn't just mad, but downright hurt, and I shouldn't be hurting. We're simply having a good time together. I shouldn't get attached. I'm not ready for a relationship, and from what Parker said, I understand that James isn't ready either. A foolish and hopeful little thought takes over: *Maybe we can help each other.*

Over the next few days, I try to concentrate on my classes, pushing this issue at the back of my mind. James calls me from his trip, but our conversation is a little awkward.

"You've been late again," Jess accuses on Friday morning, hopping through the stacks of paper and clothes lying on the floor. I'm sitting upright in my bed, holding on to my laptop for dear life.

"Yep. I was really productive, too. I sent twenty-six CVs and completed three of the crappiest online application forms ever for some investment banks in New York. If these don't lead to at least one offer I'll officially be the world's biggest loser."

"You're on the verge of a mental breakdown," she says, watching me wearily.

"No, I'm not," I protest. "That's what seniors do, apply for jobs."

They get offers too, is what I don't say out loud. Everyone around me seems to already have three offers. Everyone but me. The very top of my class and already a failure in the outside world.

Jess stares at my laptop as I tweak my CV for the next application.

"I don't understand why you don't get past the telephone interview stage. You have a perfect GPA and a kick-ass internship."

"Must be my exceptional interviewing skills," I mumble, scrolling down to the high school extracurricular activities, trying to decide which are relevant for the job and which to remove.

"God, I'll never know how you were able to do so many things in high school."

Jess's mother is the answer. When I arrived in San Francisco, and she saw the terrible depression I was in, she suggested I sign up for as many extracurricular activities as I could, to keep myself occupied. I took her advice more seriously than she expected and enrolled in literally anything that might look good on a college application.

It was exhausting, but I found that it helped me. I didn't have time to think about Kate so much. I became addicted to exhaustion, and sometimes I think I still am addicted to it.

My cell buzzes, Mum's number flashing on it.

"Hi sweetie," she greets me through heavy breathing.

"Are you training for a cross-country race? Every time you call me you sound like you've been running six miles at top speed."

"No, I was just at Ms. Evans, delivering her daughter's prom dress," she pants.

"You've been working a lot lately. Are you guys okay financially?"

I offered sending them money when I got my bookkeeping job, but Mum vehemently refused, claiming that I should focus on my studies and only work as least as possible—to cover my expenses. I will make sure it's my mother who'll work as least as possible after I graduate. Assuming I actually do find a damn job, of course.

"Don't you worry, dear. It's just a favor I've been doing for Ms. Evans."

"You've been doing a lot of favors lately, Mum."

"We're fine, honey. Really. Tell me about you. Are you all right? Is Jess taking care of you?" she asks in the soft tone that always precedes a question involving my breakup with Michael.

"Mum, I really am over Michael."

I can pass by car dealerships just fine now, without any spasm of panic. Granted, I haven't been near the one Michael worked in San Francisco ever since the breakup, but I know I'd be fine.

"Hmm," Mum says, sounding utterly unconvinced.

I sigh. "Is Dad around?"

"He's in the garden."

"What on earth are you blackmailing him with to convince him to spend so much time in the garden?" I joke.

I never got the impression that Dad was into it much. But that's the thing about Dad. There isn't much he wouldn't do to see Mum happy.

"That's just love. Honey, can I call you later? Ms. Evans just texted that I forgot my measuring tape at her place."

"Sure." She's gone the next second.

"What are you doing in my closet?" I say to Jess, who's rummaging through my dresses. She peeks behind the open door, then steps away from it holding a tiny black strapless dress—the shortest one I own. Jess gave it to me as a present. I've worn it exactly once.

"I have an announcement to make," she says.

"You're finally dyeing your hair red," I say, yawning. She's been threatening to do so since the beginning of the year.

"No, I decided I'm not yet ready for that." She throws the dress on the bed and claps her palms together, resting her chin on her fingers. "I got to the next interview round. They're flying me to London in one month."

"That's so wonderful," I cry, a little spasm of panic rushing through me as I dash off the bed and hug her. My best friend taking off… I knew she applied literally everywhere, but I always hoped we'd somehow remain near to each other.

"I would love, love, love to live in London," she says in my hair.

I let go. "You haven't even been to London, Jess."

"And I already love it. So," she puts her hands on her hips and smiles wryly, "we're going out tonight."

"What? Why?"

"To celebrate, duh."

I raise an eyebrow. "I thought we agreed to celebrate only when one of us actually gets a job."

"Well, it looks like it'll take a while until that happens, and I need a good excuse to go out."

"Like you ever need one." I smile, ridiculously

happy for my friend.

"Well no, but you do," she says.

"You just told me yesterday that you're broke. I'm not doing spectacularly well, either."

"One night out won't make that much of a difference."

“I had planned to send more applications tonight.”

Along with all my prayers, a voodoo doll, and anything else that might help elicit a positive response.

“You can send them tomorrow. It’s Saturday, so no one will read them until Monday anyway. It won’t make a difference when you send them. So, we’re going out tonight. Do you mind if I borrow this?" She points at the tiny piece of black fabric on the bed.

“Not at all.”

CHAPTER NINE

I'm wearing a black dress too. It's short, though not as short as Jess's, and I feel sexy in it. We're standing in line, waiting to enter the club she chose.

"I can't believe the idiot wouldn't let us in." Jess stomps her foot, glaring at the doorman. We went directly to him when we arrived, with Jess flaunting her most charming smile, which usually gets us in anywhere without having to wait in the line. Not in this case.

"I can't believe we are celebrating your trip to London in this place."

"The cheapskates we are meeting chose the location. Besides, we can't afford to be picky. At least this place is cheap."

"As long as whatever they put in their cocktails is FDA approved," I mumble to myself.

We stand in line for five minutes before we enter the club, Jess pointedly looking in the other direction when we pass the doorman. The place is just as run-down as I remember it from three years ago, when I spent exactly one hour inside before fleeing. For Jess's sake, I'll try longer this time.

"Do we know where everyone is?" I ask as we descend the shabby staircase to the dance floor, the bass rhythm drumming in my ears already.

Jess gestures me to follow her as we reach the dance floor. It's not as packed as it should be on a Saturday night, and when we arrive at the bar, I understand why. Everyone, our group included, is hovering along the counter, desperately trying to get the attention of the bartender. Four of Jess's classmates, two guys and two girls, are among them. I only know one of the guys personally—Jason, from the volleyball team.

Jason slips away from the group when he sees me. "I didn't know you were coming." He bends down to kiss me on both cheeks. "You look great," he adds, doing a lousy job at hiding his astonishment. I can't blame him. All Jason has ever seen me wearing are baggy T-shirts, shorts, and messy buns or ponytails. He, on the other hand, with his striking green eyes and six-pack visible under no matter what he is wearing, never looked anything other than hot.

"Thanks."

"What do you want to drink?" Jess yells at me from the bar.

"Just Sprite," I call.

She purses her lips. "You promised."

I really did promise her a toast. I'm the only one she told about the job interview so she can't celebrate with anyone other than me.

"Nothing too strong, please—with Red Bull in it."

"It'll take a while before any of us gets a drink," Jason says, flashing a smile as a new song starts. "Let's dance."

"Umm… I'd rather not," I say nervously and his smile drops. "I'm not very good."

I look around, astounded to find Dani in the crowd. What is she doing here? She sees me too and waves at me frantically. Parker appears beside her a second later.

Jason comes closer, until he's practically glued to me. "You look really fantastic tonight," he says in my ear and one of his hands moves to my hip. I step back.

"Come on, let's dance."

"No."

"But—"

"She said no," a deep voice booms from behind me. James.

"Who the hell are you?" Jason says over my shoulder.

His jaw is tight, his elbows wide away from his torso in a provoking way. The dark blue shirt reminds me of the one he was wearing when we first met.

"This is James," I say at once because I have the nagging feeling James is preparing to punch Jason rather than answering his question. "A friend of mine."

"Sure."

I stride toward the bar, with James hot on my heels. I look for Jess, but she and the rest of the group are no longer where I left them.

"James, this is a surprise. When did you return?"

"A few hours ago."

"How did you know where I was?"

He hesitates, then his gaze slips sideways to Jess.

"You spoke to her?"

He nods, smiling. "I wanted to surprise you tonight."

Hmmm…by showing up here?

"Can we go outside and talk? It's loud in here."

"Sure."

We walk outside, where the line is twice as long as when Jess and I were waiting. A bunch of giggling girls stare at James, taking him in from head to toe when we pass them, my existence not deterring them in the slightest.

I walk around the corner, and except for a few garbage cans, it's just us.

"You sounded strange on the phone when we spoke," James says.

"I know…so did you though."

"I'm sorry I upset you."

"No, I'm sorry for jumping to conclusions. I don't know why I overreacted…"

"You were jealous." He's smiling.

I poke his chest. "That amuses you?"

"It means you like me."

I poke him again. "Of course I like you. You give me amazing orgasms. And you make me laugh." *And you bring me comfort when I'm sad.*

"I like being with you, Serena. Spending time together. This…all this is new to me. I haven't dated like a normal person in years, but I'd like to try it with you." His words take my breath away. When he puts his arms around me, bringing me closer, my body feels like a livewire. "Say something."

"James, my last relationship ended badly. I don't know if I'm ready."

He swallows, nodding. "I don't know if I am either. Why don't we both take a risk?"

He raises one of his hands and tucks a strand of hair behind my ear. His hand has a slight tremor to it. His whole body has. "I want you to be mine. Only mine."

I nod, and then his lips touch mine in a fierce kiss. My whole body responds to it with a frantic desire to touch and kiss every inch of him. His lips descend on my neck and my chest. He reaches the neckline of my dress and pulls it down in one swift move, revealing one of my breasts. His tongue around my nipple sends me over the edge with a loud moan.

"No, James, please," I beg, pulling him up and rearranging my dress. Then I launch into another kiss, fiercer than the first one. My hands find their way under his shirt and he's the one moaning when my fingers almost scratch his skin.

We stop, gasping, our foreheads together. He pushes away my hands from under his shirt, saying, "Stop, or I'll have you right here."

He takes a step back, putting one finger against his lips, now curled into an uneven smile.

"Let's leave this place."

"I actually promised Jess I would celebrate with her something."

"I know. She said she'd be happy to celebrate another time when I told her about the surprise I prepared for you."

"You prepared a… surprise?" I ask blankly.

"Of course. You didn't think I plotted with her

to just show up here?"

"I…wow. I don't know what to say."

"You don't have to say anything. Just trust me."

I smile, sighing. "Well, if we have Jess's blessing, let's go."

CHAPTER TEN

The Porsche is parked opposite the club and when I slip inside, butterflies start to lazily flutter their wings in my stomach. James slips inside and starts the engine, then starts rummaging in the pocket of the door. Just when I'm about to ask him what he's looking for, he pulls out a thin strip of black silk.

"You have to put this on."

"A blindfold? Are you serious?"

"Very."

"James, I'm not putting this on."

"Then we are not going anywhere," he says and actually turns off the engine.

"I don't know where we're going anyway."

"Why do you protest so much, then?" he asks, his lip curling into a smile. He forms a semicircle in the air with his forefinger and I turn around, sighing.

The flutter of butterflies isn't lazy anymore when the fine silk touches my skin and his fingers become entangled in my hair as he ties the piece of fabric.

"This is ridiculous," I say.

"The blindfold matches your dress," he says amused. "By the way, what were you thinking wearing something this provocative?"

"You don't like it?" I tease.

"You look great in it. A little too great." He glides one finger playfully up my thigh, sending delicious little tingles in my entire body. "You're tan."

"I played volleyball in the sun almost the entire day. How long will this ride last?"

"About an hour," he says as he starts the car.

"Wow—“

A buzzing noise interrupts me and I clumsily try to open my tiny bag to reach my phone.

"Leave it, it's my phone."

He snorts after a few seconds. "Dani's checking whether I'm off with you. Well, she only misspelled two words, so I guess she's still sober." The concern behind his mocking tone is not lost on me.

"Don't worry. Parker will take good care of her."

"

"I hope so. Dani is determined not to be a bookworm anymore when she arrives at Oxford, and apparently she needs six months of clubbing to achieve that."

"Why are you worried?"

"I don't want her to waste her time at Oxford crawling from party to party," he exclaims.

"That's a bit hypocritical coming from someone who ravaged his entire trust fund in college."

"It actually only took me three years. I was already broke by the fourth year. But she's got no reason to be as reckless as I was. "

The words are past my lips before I fully realize what I'm saying. "Was Lara your reason?"

I whisk the blindfold off, but he doesn't notice. His faze is fixed on the road ahead.

"How do you know about her?"

"Umm… Parker sort of—"

He grunts.

"Don't get mad at him. It sort of slipped."

"What *exactly* slipped?"

"That she… died at your high school graduation," I say in a small voice.

Neither of us speaks for a few seconds. I try to gauge something, anything from his expression, but it's completely unreadable as he looks forward.

"You'd think that would have been the worst

day of my life. But the days after it were much worse. The years, really."

I know what he means. At first the shock makes you numb. The pain comes later.

"I went into sort of a nightmare afterward and only woke up from it when the balance on my account hit zero."

"James you don't have to tell me these things. I just—I'm sorry I brought this up."

"No, it's fine." He looks at me with a kind, warm smile. "My dad, understandably, cut off any financial aid, so I started working the summer before senior year. Found out it drained me more than partying, so I took on as much as possible."

Ah, addiction to work and exhaustion. One more thing we have in common besides the obsession with movies.

"Much more constructive," I say in an attempt to cheer us up.

"You've dealt with things in a constructive way right from the beginning," he says and I detect admiration in his voice.

"Everyone copes in their own way," I say quietly. I sink in my seat as I realize the speed indicator is so far to the right I can't see it at all anymore. "When you said one hour did you mean three hours for normal drivers?"

He smirks. "One of the reasons I thought a

blindfold might be useful. By the way, put that back on."

"But I already know you're driving like a maniac," I protest.

"I said that was just one of the reasons." His smirk accelerates along with the car. "We're almost there so I really want you to put that on."

"Fine," I say and I start tying the silk, twitching as I accidentally pull a few strands of hair.

A sharp curve to the right tells me that we are leaving the highway.

"And we're here," James announces a few minutes later. I sit up straight in my seat, pointing my ears as the car slows down and then comes to a halt. A muffled sound comes from outside, like metal scratching. A gate opening, maybe? My guess is confirmed when we start moving again, at a slow pace. We stop again almost immediately and this time I hear James turn off the engine. He gets out of the car without a word. A few seconds later, he (or at least I hope it's James) opens my door. I expect him to take my hand and guide me out, but he lifts me in his arms.

"This is bordering on creepy," I giggle.

"Your faith in me is astounding," James says.

I barely manage to take in a few deep breaths of the warm, evening air when we step into a closed space. A weirdly smelling one too. Good weird.

There's a slightly sweet aroma lingering in the air. An aroma I know. An aroma I love.

Chocolate.

It's a few more steps before James finally puts me down and takes my blindfold off. I stare at the long corridor in front of us confused. There's no chocolate in sight. Only plastic containers, like over-sized liquid soap dispensers lined up on each side, and giant glass windows through which huge metal cans and pipes are visible.

"I know you love chocolate. I thought you'd appreciate this. We can taste everything," James says from behind me.

"Oh wow," I exclaim, realizing that those containers don't have soap in them but chocolate.

We're in a chocolate factory.

I swirl around and throw my arms around his neck, pulling him in a tight embrace. "How is this possible?" I ask, unable to stop my legs from jiggling with nervous excitement.

"A friend of mine owns the factory," he says when I finally step back, allowing him to breathe. "He wants to add a museum to it, to show the process, offer tastings and everything. It won't open for another month or so, so you're their unofficial test customer."

"Fantastic," I say, turning toward the corridor.

"The machines," he points to the huge metal

cans behind the windows, "are actually closed at night but I told him you'd care only about the tasting part any way."

"You know me well."

"What are you waiting for? Dig in. And feel free to ignore me, I won't mind."

There is a bowl with mini waffles next to each chocolate dispenser. I grab one and hold it under the first dispenser, pushing the big round button on it. A dark reddish-brown cream decorates my waffle.

"Oh my God. Hot cherry chocolate," I say, shoving the entire waffle in my mouth. "This is a dream come true."

I fill another waffle and wave in front of James's lips, "Come on, just one bite."

"I'm really okay," he says and actually takes a step back.

"How can you be in chocolate paradise and not taste anything?"

"One of the perks of not being a big chocolate fan," he smirks. I shrug and eat the tiny piece of heaven myself. I make a grab for a third waffle but James says, "I'd suggest you don't empty the cherry supply. You've got plenty of others to taste."

"Thanks for saving me from myself," I joke while proceeding to the next dispenser.

Fifteen mini waffles later, and strawberry, raspberry, banana, pineapple, currant, caramel, cinnamon, mocchacino, cappuccino, chili, and so many kinds of pepper chocolate I keep mixing up their names, there's not one type of chocolate in the room I haven't tasted.

I take a deep breath and make a mental note to only use half a waffle for each container as we step into the next room. It's twice as long as the one we left behind. There are no waffles next to the dispensers. The dispensers aren't like the other ones either. Through the glass tops I can clearly see that the chocolate inside each is solid. I press the lever under the dispenser and a long slim piece of chocolate falls in the tray next to it.

By the time we reach the last room, which is part of the museum-to-be, I can hardly breathe. We've been in one room where chocolates were arranged according to how much milk they have inside, one according to how many different flavors there are, and one where I got to mix my own personal chocolate drink.

"I am officially stoned on chocolate," I say, as James opens the door. My jaw drops. I step inside, glancing incredulously to my left and then to my right. A melted chocolate river flows on each side. Of course they kept what is best for last. There is a basket full of regular-sized waffles on the table between the two rivulets.

"Are you saying what I'm thinking?" James asks.

"Depends what you're thinking."

"That you can't eat anymore."

"That's really the only thing you are thinking about?" I ask playfully.

"That and everything else I still have planned for tonight." He bites his lip.

"Tell me."

"I'll do something better. I'll show you if you're done here."

"You think I'd leave this place without tasting the chocolate rivers?" I ask with fake horror. I grab a waffle and a paper plate then dip half in one river, and the other half in the second one, resulting in my fingers getting as dirty as a three-year-old's when left alone with a chocolate cake.

"I just don't think I'll be able to eat more than a waffle." I do my best to eat up all the chocolate on my fingers.

He laughs softly, wrapping his arms around me from behind and placing small, delicious kisses on the side of my neck.

"James," I murmur, as soft bites replace the kisses, and delicious tingles take over my entire body. I put down the plate and turn around and kiss him.

Or attempt to, because this thing we are doing

doesn't really do justice to the concept of kissing. It's clumsy and weird and I have the strange feeling he's trying to hold back.

"What's wrong?" I ask.

"Nothing."

"The first kiss I had in sixth grade was less awkward than this, and there was a lot of teeth clashing involved. Tell me what's wrong."

"I'll bring this up another time, eat your waffle."

"James," I press.

He takes a deep breath. "I've been meaning to ask you this but I didn't know how. Do you still have feelings for your ex?"

"Yes. I want to kick him in the balls repeatedly."

He chuckles, but I can sense that he still feels uneasy. "That's not what I mean. If he showed up and tried to make amends or something, would you give him a chance?"

"What? No. I don't want anything to do with him."

"You're sure?"

"Yes."

He nods. "Okay. Because I don't want to just be your rebound."

"James…" I take his handsome face between my hands, kissing his jaw. "You're not. I mean, I admit that's what I thought this was in the beginning, but since our weekend together, I realized it was more."

"Are you saying this because you're afraid I might not let you eat your waffle if you don't?" His tone is playful, but his frown doesn't dissipate entirely.

"Maybe." I play with the top button of his shirt. "Or maybe it's the truth."

"It'd better be," he caresses my lips with his thumb. "Because I really want to give this a shot. In fact, I want it so much that it scares me."

He kisses me softly, until I melt in his arms.

"You aren't going to eat that waffle any time soon, are you?" he says when we stop to breathe.

"Why? Are we in a hurry?" I turn to my waffle. "What's next? A trip to the moon?"

"I was thinking of something less ambitious," he murmurs in my ear, perusing his hand over my thigh, pulling up my dress, "like making love."

"Mmm… I thought that might come up," I tease, leaning my head on his shoulder. "Am I allowed to take more waffles with me for later?"

"If that's the price," he says.

"I'll be faster if you help me. Come on, grab a waffle."

We both head to the river carrying one. I also take my plate with me. "No chance for you to taste the chocolate?" I ask as I dip my waffle in the chocolate.

"Nope."

I set my waffle aside on the plate on top of the old one.

"Not even if I put it here?" I say, lowering my dress so one nipple shows. I smear chocolate around it with my fingers. He raises his head slowly, biting his lower lip. I dip my fingers in chocolate again and do the same with the other nipple, looking him in the eyes the whole time. A rivulet of sweat oozes on his temple. I lower my eyes to his the bulge in his pants, and the craving inside me awakens instantly. I'm the one biting my lip now, though he hasn't moved one inch closer to me. I start lowering my dress more and more. And now he does step closer. I let out a moan when his tongue comes in contact with my nipple. He circles it again and again, until all the chocolate is gone and I'm more aroused than ever.

"So you do eat chocolate," I tease, though my voice is nothing more than a whisper.

"Depends how it's served," he utters against my skin.

He moves over to the other nipple and I cry, pulling at his hair, "I want you James."

His fingers trail up on my inner thigh.

"Touch me, please," I beg.

"You're so wet," he says, touching my sex through my panties. I press against his fingers, in a silent imploration for him to remove the damn panties.

He doesn't. He removes his fingers completely instead, rising. He is trembling, his erection against me. I lower my hand and he swallows hard when I touch him.

"No, Serena," he breathes against my lips. "I don't want to have you here, like this." He covers my hand with his, but doesn't remove it. "I want tonight to be different. Special."

I look up at him in surprise, then smile. He removes my hand, a sign that whatever plan he has for us is one touch away from crumbling. I take a step back, pulling up my dress.

"Let's go, then," I say.

He takes my hand. I grab the plate with waffles with my other hand as he drags me after him.

CHAPTER ELEVEN

"**W**here are we going?" I ask, struggling to keep my plate from bouncing too violently. The last thing I want is my for waffles to land on the floor.

"Somewhere where we'll be comfortable."

"The floor between the rivers looked comfortable enough," I say, feeling my face getting all hot. I increase my pace, despite the fact that my heels are killing me. A few minutes into our jog, we leave the factory premises behind and enter an office building.

"Wow, these really look comfortable," I say sarcastically, staring at the open space, full of desks and chairs. "And special. How's this better than the factory?"

"There is no one here."

"What?" I ask, suddenly out of breath. "There were people . . . in the factory?"

He finally stops and I take up the opportunity to lean on a desk and give my feet some relief.

"Don't worry, no one was watching us," he says, leaning on the door in front of me. "You didn't think that those rivers would just run the entire night, did you?"

"Right," I mumble. I hadn't given any thought to that. "What friend owns this who would just hand you the keys so we can barge inside in the middle of the night?"

"My family," he smirks.

"You've got your own chocolate factory?" I grin. "You just became the runner-up to being the most awesome person ever."

"Who's got first place?"

"Like I'd tell you."

"Then maybe this will get me number one," he says and pushes open the door behind him.

I expect to find a fancy office, possibly with a mahogany desk and maybe even a lush couch. James doesn't turn on any light, so the only wisp of light in the pitch dark comes from outside the corridor. But it's enough for me to realize that the room couldn't look less like an office.

There is a large bed in the middle of the room—an air mattress, I suspect, but I can't be sure with all the silky covers on it.

James takes my hand and leads me to the bed,

gesturing me to sit on it. It really is an air mattress. I watch confused as he walks over to a cabinet. For a few moments I think he's searching for something on its surface, and then I gasp, because he steps aside, revealing a candle. One by one, he lights up twelve candles around the room. My heart gives a jolt with each tiny flame, and I can't do anything but stare at him because I am truly at a loss for words.

When he returns, I get up and put my arms around his neck.

"This is perfect," I manage to say.

"You are all I've ever wanted. I want to get lost in you."

One of his arms slides up my back and he unzips my dress. I feel like I'm back on that plane, with the door open. Ready to plunge. Ready to abandon myself in the free fall, with no one to trust but him.

***

I pull the cover over my head as the bright sunlight stabs my eyes without mercy.

"Morning," a voice calls from somewhere. I stretch my arm and a painful twinge pierces my heart. There's no one beside me. I'm imagining his voice. I imagined everything and am actually in my bed, probably passed out from too much work.

But it can't be. The mattress is too soft, the sheets too delicate.

I lower the cover slowly, very slowly, and find James at the foot of the mattress, fully dressed.

"Come on, we've got a long day ahead of us," he grins.

"Just give me a minute," I grumble. "I can't think without a cup of coffee."

"The faster we leave, the faster you'll get coffee."

"I need my phone," I say, pressing the bottom of my palms on my eyes.

A soft thump next to my ear tells me I don't have to search for it anymore. I always read one or two random news articles right after waking up, just to give my eyes something to do so they don't shut themselves again. Of course, the past few days I skipped that in favor of obsessively checking my emails for replies from the myriad of applications I sent. And even though it's Sunday, I open my mailbox instead of browsing on news sites.

I instantly leap in a sitting position. "I can't believe this," I yelp.

"You won the lottery?" James chuckles.

"I just received a rejection." I stare at the email in disbelief. "It's not even one of those automatic replies. Someone actually took his time to write this on a Sunday. Man, they must have really hated me. Who the hell sends rejection emails on a Sunday?"

"Somebody you don't want to work for, trust me," James says.

I smile, repeating to myself, as I do every time such an email arrives, that it's not that much of a setback. I've still got tons of applications out.

“You should really make use of your computer science minor and apply for jobs in that area as well. It would widen your options.”

I sigh. This is something I’ve tried very hard to avoid, since I’m not really into computer science at all. I was just too proud to drop it as a minor. But I know James is right. And anything is better than flipping burgers.

James seats himself next to me, holding up the paper plate. There's only one waffle on it.

"You ate one of my waffles," I accuse. I decide not to bring up the email again. There are a million more pleasant things I can say and do on my first day as… his girlfriend, as he called me last night before we both fell asleep. Just saying the word to myself brings a warm, fluttering feeling. Just in my stomach at first, but then it spreads up to my chest and throat with a dazzling, elevating power. I wonder how weird it would look if I would suddenly hug him now.

Very weird, probably, so I just sit back, taking in as much of him as my eyes allow.

"I'm starving," he says.

I take a bite, but the cold waffle tastes a hundred times more disappointing than I imagined it would when I decided last night I was really too full and that I'd better leave it for breakfast.

"You do know I can't go anywhere dressed in that in broad daylight, don't you?" I point to the black dress on the floor, because his impatient smirk tells me he has the whole day planned out.

He kisses me sweet and soft.

"Wearing nothing suits you best anyway," he says mockingly when we break off, taking another bite from the waffle.

I stick out my tongue, and grudgingly get out of bed. It takes me about five minutes to get fully dressed, and by the time I'm done, I feel more naked than when I had nothing on.

"Should we clean up?" I ask, looking around at the melted candles.

"The cleaning personnel will do it. Let's go."

I take one last look at the room from the doorway, wishing to remember every detail; the sanctuary of the first night in which our kisses and caresses were preludes to much more than reckless passion.

As if knowing what I'm thinking, he whispers in

my ear, "There will be more nights like this, I promise."

I smile and let him drag me through the sea of desks.

My phone starts buzzing when we reach the car, and I manage to get it as I slide in the car.

Jess is calling. I press answer just as James starts the engine and the voice at the other end of the invisible line instantly alerts me that there's something wrong. Very, very wrong.

"Parker? Why do you have Jess's phone?"

"Don't panic, please," he says in a tone that screams for me to panic. "I'm with her at the hospital."

A paralyzing coldness takes over.

It's only after a long pause that I manage to mumble, "What happened to her?"

"She got involved with a moron last night… I'll explain everything when you get here."

I dig my nails deep into my palm. "Which hospital are you in?"

"The one where you volunteer. We're on the fourth floor."

"I'll be there as soon as possible."

I close the phone and turn to a concerned James. "How fast can you drive?"

I barely feel James's arm over my shoulders as

we walk inside the hospital some time later. I am numb with fear. I stopped hearing him a while ago in the car.

Dani greets us as we get out of the elevator on the fourth floor.

"Where's Jess?" I ask.

"They're doing her some tests right now, you can't see her," Dani says.

"What happened?" James asks, looking at Dani concerned, scanning her as if checking to see if she has all her limbs.

"I don't know," Dani mumbles, staring at her feet.

"Dani?" I press.

"I really don't. I was outside the club talking to... someone."

James instantly tenses up.

"Yes, a guy," I say impatiently. "Please continue."

"There was some kind of fight inside the club."

"The moron Jessica was dancing with started it," Parker says, appearing from a narrow corridor. "The whole place was in chaos before long."

I gasp. He's got a black eye, and his lower lip is split.

"What happened to Jess?" I ask.

Parker looks from James to me, then says quietly. "She fell through a glass wall behind the bar. There was a ladder on the other side."

I cover my mouth with both hands. James puts a comforting arm around me.

"How is she now?" he asks.

"No idea," Parker says, obviously frustrated. "They won't tell you anything if you're not part of the family. The doctor talked to her mother, but she doesn't seem capable of talking."

"Jess's mother is here?"

"I found her number in Jess's phone and called her," Dani explains.

"I think you should talk to her," Parker says.

Dani looks at me wide-eyed, balancing from one foot to the other. I nod. She leads me through the labyrinth of corridors until we reach a waiting room, where Jess's mother is alone.

She's curled into a seat, her thin frame looking more fragile than ever. She's staring into space, twisting a strand of hair between her fingers.

"Mrs. Haydn?" I call, sitting next to her.

"My poor girl," she says almost inaudibly.

I take her free hand between my palms and rub it energetically because it's ice cold.

"What did the doctor tell you?"

"Two broken ribs, and her left leg is fractured. I saw her before they took her for some more tests, I never—"

"Where is Mr. Haydn?" I interrupt, because her

voice trembles to the point of breaking.

"His boss couldn't find someone to replace his Sunday shift so he didn't allow him to take the day off." She breaks into tears.

I put my arm around her shoulders in a tender embrace.

James's voice makes me leap to my feet. He's walking toward us, accompanied by a doctor—a tall, balding man in a white coat, carrying a thin file under his arm. Dani trails in silence behind them. Mrs. Haydn stands up too beside me.

"You can see your daughter now, Mrs. Haydn," the doctor says.

"How is she?" I ask him as James comes by my side, gently squeezing my hand in a silent encouragement.

"She will make a full recovery. But it will take some time," he answers in an official, not unkind tone.

I turn to Ms. Haydn, expecting to find her as relieved as I feel but her expression hasn't relaxed one bit.

"Mrs. Haydn, do you want to go see Jess?" I ask.

She looks at me terrified, as if I'd asked her to walk on burning coal. "You go first, my dear. I'll go right after you."

"Okay," I stutter, looking questioningly at the doctor. He gestures for me to follow him and after a brief hesitation, I do.

"Please take care of her," I whisper to James over my shoulder.

We don't walk for long before the doctor stops, in front of a door. "She is still asleep now. Please remember, it looks worse than it really is."

On that cheery note, he takes off. I stare after him for a few seconds, then take a deep breath and push the door open. One glance at the bed and I understand Mrs. Haydn's horror at the thought of seeing Jess. Any part of her body that isn't covered in white bandages is bruised. There is a long, slim bandage on her cheek, and I dearly pray it won't leave a scar behind. How could this happen to her? I should have never agreed to go to that godforsaken tap house. I should have never left her alone there with that bunch of idiots. I caress her non-bandaged cheek, reminding myself that the doctor said it looks worse than it really is.

I can't help but think about my sister. My dearest Kate. But Jess isn't Kate. She'll get out of the hospital, and probably limp for a while and certainly be cranky, but she'll be all right. I just wish she'd be awake already.

I brush my tears away and leave the room without a last glance at her. Stupid and absurd as it is, I can't stop the tears from forming behind my eyelids when I look at her.

Her mum is leaning against the wall outside the room. To my relief, she looks like her usual self.

"She's still asleep," I say.

"Oh, the doctor said she'll be asleep for a few more hours. I'll just wait by her side until she wakes up."

"Do you need me to bring you anything?"

"Thanks, dear. Your boyfriend already asked. I'm fine."

"Oh, my boyfriend," I stutter.

"He seems like a nice boy."

I stare her. It took her two years for her to finally stop frowning whenever I mentioned Michael. "You don't know him."

"No, but he just ran six blocks to get you Starbucks coffee." She points to something behind me. "That's enough to earn him *nice* in my book."

I turn around and find James sitting in one of the chairs in the waiting room, carrying two coffee cups and a paper bag.

"Go to him honey," she beckons, "you look like you haven't had coffee today."

"I certainly haven't," I say.

"Dani and Parker went to your place to get you something to change into and bring some stuff for Jess. How is she?" James asks when I get to him, handing me the bag.

"Looks horrible, but she'll be fine." I open the

brown paper bag. There is a grilled vegetable sandwich inside. "I'm glad Mrs. Haydn is holding up so well. She scared me a little before." I take a bite from the sandwich and a few sips of coffee. "I'll just stay here for whatever she needs."

"And I'll be here for whatever you need," James says, holding up my chin.

"Thanks," I say deeply moved.

"You want to go in there again with her mom?"

"No," I say a little too quickly. "I mean, I don't really… I'll go in when Jess wakes up." I bite into my sandwich again, avoiding his gaze.

"It's all right, you know," James says kindly. "To think about Kate."

He pulls me in his arms, and I swear, there is no better place in the world. It's a safe haven.

CHAPTER TWELVE

I spend the next two days running from Starbucks to Jess's room and back. Jess is, as I predicted, in the crankiest mood ever. She insisted on the nurse taking off the bandage on her cheek so she could inspect her wound. She became even crankier afterward.

Her mum is doing remarkably well, taking regular naps on the couch in Jess's room. I tried it too, but my back hurts so badly when I lie on it, I've given up on sleeping altogether. Her dad comes to visit in the evening, after he gets off from work.

James hasn't left my side at all, and is now chanting apology after apology because he has to leave for a meeting with investors he absolutely can't postpone.

"I'll be back in four hours at the latest," he says.

"I'll be fine. Please go home and sleep after your meeting is over James. I can take carc of myself."

"Not a chance."

He leans in and brushes my lips in what was supposed to be a quick kiss. But it transforms, as every kiss did in the past two days, into a deep, longing one.

"Hurry," I say when we break off. "You won't impress any investor if you don't have time to shower before showing up at the meeting."

"You could use a shower yourself," he jokes, but I immediately feel uncomfortable. I've been wearing the clothes Dani brought me from the apartment for two days.

He cups my face in his palms and kisses my forehead once before disappearing in an elevator.

The other elevator doors open a few seconds later. At first I think it's empty, then a tiny figure skids out of it. Barefoot, the blue hospital gown far too large for her small body, she's clutching her storybook against her chest. Six year old Maya, one of the little girls I volunteer for.

"Maya, what are you doing here?" I say and take her in my arms not wanting her to get sick from wandering without shoes on the cold floors. I immediately take her to the chairs and slump in one of them, rubbing my back.

"I heard nurse Mary say that you were here," she says, putting her tiny arms around my neck. "Why didn't you come to see me? Are you mad at me because I put cake in your hair at the party?"

I cannot help a smile. "I'm not mad at you at all. I had to take care of other things but I was going to come see you."

"Are you sick?" she says with a frown.

"A friend of mine is."

"Don't be sad. Look, this will make you happy." She clutches her book around her chest. "Will you read me a story?" she asks, looking at me with wide, hopeful eyes.

"Let's go upstairs and I'll read to all of you."

She doesn't answer right away, and I understand the conflict that is going on inside her. There are two sides to Maya. One that allows her to share all the candies she receives from her parents with all the other girls in her ward, and the other side that wants things—usually my attention—only for herself.

"Can we stay here?" she asks in a small, small voice. "Just for one story?"

I pretend to be thinking hard. "Does anyone know you are here?"

"No," she says. "But I don't think they'll notice. I left immediately after nurse Mary left and she won't come for another hour."

I eye her closely. "Just one story."

She opens the book to her favorite story: Cinderella. I must have read it to her at least fifteen times. She leans her head against my chest and I start reading in a loud voice, because the waiting room is empty.

I realize Maya has fallen asleep when I finish the story.

"You should be a professional storyteller."

I raise my head so fast my neck snaps painfully.

"Parker," I blurt. I haven't seen him since I first arrived at the hospital, since he's been busy taking all of James's meetings. His black eye is almost healed. So is his lip. "How long have you been standing here?"

"Not that long," he says with a smile. "Shouldn't we take her to bed?"

"Yeah we should."

"I'll do it."

"There she is," someone exclaims, walking with heavy steps toward us. Nurse Mary. "I knew she'd come to see you. Give her to me, I'll take her upstairs."

Nurse Mary has been working here for as long as I can remember. She changes her haircut at least once a month, and the hair color every six months. The shockingly short, red do, styled in messy spikes with far too much hair gel, is her most endearing experiment yet.

"I'm sorry I didn't pass by to see the girls," I whisper, placing Maya in her arms with great care.

"Please, Serena. I know you're here for your friend. Let me know if there's anything I can do for you."

"That's very kind of you," I murmur as she takes off with Maya.

I turn to Parker, who sits in the chair next to me. "Did James send you?" It's so like James not to trust that I'd be all right by myself.

"No, I came by myself," Parker answers with fake affronting. "To visit Jessica. But James will be back after the meeting. He just can't stay away. You're good for him."

"I don't know about that," I say jokingly, "but he's good for me."

Good is an understatement, really. The best, the perfect one. Now that he's only mine and I am his, there's no reason not to admit he's perfect for me.

Except for that one not-so-little bug I can't get rid of—I'm by far not perfect for him.

"I just don't get what he sees in me," I voice my fear aloud for the first time.

Parker looks at me kindly, with blue eyes that resemble James's too much. "You're different from the women around him."

"I know that I'm not one of *you*," I say,

remembering Natalie's comment. "I don't go on expensive trips in Malaysia or—"

"No," he interrupts, "you work your arse off—pardon my expression—and in your free time do things like this." He raises his hand in the direction nurse Mary left with Maya.

"Oh stop acting like you're impressed or something. You attend charity balls for God's sake."

"Yeah," he says warily, "organized by women who have too much time and money on their hands. Don't get me wrong, I respect Aunt Beatrix, but charity is what they do. It's required of them. It's what Natalie and Angela and all others will do after they get married."

"Stuck in the past century much?"

He frowns. "Not really. They all have a choice. They can choose to work, like Christie, and strive on their own. They just don't want that."

I stare at him, and have the impression this is the first time I really see him. By the courteous way he always addresses the lark, I would've never guessed what he really thinks of her. I wonder if I wasn't too quick in thinking that he likes me. I don't think I was.

"I thought Natalie owned part of your and James's company," I say.

"She does. A small part. But she's not really

involved in anything. Just passes by the office from time to time. I think she wanted to get involved just for fun, and because she likes to tell people she has something to do. Though investors seem to like her very much," Parker says with an expression that tells me he questions the sanity of the investors.

I cannot hold back a smile. "So, want to go in and see Jess?"

"I should. She made me promise in the bar before the whole mayhem started that I'd tell her a few things about London."

I bite my tongue to stop myself from laughing, pondering whether I should tell him that a few things are synonymous with one hell of an interrogation round. I decide against it. When I offered to give her tips on things to do in London, she blatantly told me she needs another source of information because I left London such a long time ago all my tips would be outdated. She's probably right.

"Yeah, she had to reschedule that interview because she's going to have that cast on her leg for quite a while. Her room is that way." I point with my thumb to my right. "Just don't tell her you came here by car. She'll try to make you drive her around."

I brought her car here yesterday, thinking I

might need it in case James eventually had to leave. When she saw the car keys, she begged me for half an hour to take her for a ride, claiming she couldn't bear lying in bed anymore. I tuck the keys safely away from her in my jeans ever since.

"I thought she seemed a little nuts in the bar," he winks and I burst out laughing, elbowing him.

"That's a very rude thing to say."

"Well, this will sound even more rude," he puts an arm over my shoulder, and I lean in, curiously. "I think she—"

“Parker, you’re here,” James interrupts. Parker leans back instantly.

"James, you're back early," I say, shocked. It's not his return that shocks me, but the way he looks between me and Parker. Like he’s *jealous.*

What the hell?

I expect Parker to react somehow, but he asks in a tone that couldn't be more natural, "How did the meeting go?"

"They canceled," James answers and I’m relieved that his voice almost sounds normal. "I suited up for nothing." He undoes his tie. "We rescheduled for tomorrow."

Parker frowns. "In the afternoon, I hope? You can't postpone the meeting with the agency in the morning."

"It's in the afternoon, but you go to the meeting

with the agency," James says.

"Don't miss it on my account," I say.

He lifts my chin with his fingers. "You're far more important than any meeting." He drops his voice to a whisper. "You're more important than anything."

"I'll go inside to Jess," Parker says. "Remind me to finish that story later, Serena."

James leans in to kiss me after Parker is gone, but I pull back. I am not as willing as Parker to let the matter go so easily.

"What was that?"

"What do you mean?" he asks, but the way his head jerks up and his jaw tights, he knows exactly what I am talking about.

"Your Othello reaction when you saw Parker."

"It wasn't that bad," he says, and the smile he now flashes is truly forced.

"Yes it was," I insist. "You are seriously jealous of your cousin?"

Sweat breaks out on his forehead. "Serena, can we please drop this?"

"Why? I don't want you to feel like you have to be jealous of anyone. Especially Parker."

"I know." He takes both my hands and pulls me in a gentle embrace, burying his head in my neck. "I know you're mine. Only mine." His words send shivers down my spine. The wrong kind of shivers.

He sounds as if he's trying to convince himself of the fact that I really am only his. His heartbeats reverberate against my chest in violent, lightning quick drums that betray an inner turmoil he's trying to cover up.

"What's wrong, James?"

He shakes his head. "I'll tell you another time."

"You promise?"

"Yes."

He stays at the hospital for another hour, but I can't make this strangeness between us go away. My heart is heavy when he leaves, wondering how I can make him open up. I don't want to push him, but I think he needs it.

***

Next day, Jess is discharged, and I take her home. Over the next week, her mood improves drastically, even though she moves slowly with her cast. James visits us every evening for dinner, and even Parker stops by from time to time.

"Is it my impression, or are Jess and Parker getting along really well?" I whisper to James, pulling him away from those two. "Jess even said he stopped by during the day."

James whistles. "That would be something."

"Do you want to stay the night?" I wiggle my

eyebrows.

James wiggles them back. "I thought you'd never ask."

"Oh, I see. So you dropped by for dinner every day this week just on the off-chance you might get laid?" I tease.

"Of course not. I like spending time with you. But getting in your pants is a definite bonus."

I elbow him playfully. "This is your lucky night, Cohen."

After Parker leaves, I help Jess to her room, and then James and I have the living room to ourselves. We're on the couch, and the man is kissing me like he's been starving for my lips for days.

"I love this," he says. "Spending time with you in the evening. Knowing I can come to you," he whispers when he moves to my neck. "You make me so happy, Serena."

"I'm glad for that. But...I can feel that you're tense about something."

He stills, his ragged breath heating up my neck.

"Sometimes I wonder if I'm good enough for you."

Wow. I wasn't expecting this.

"Why would you say that? Does it have to do with what happened at the hospital with Parker?"

James settles next to me, swallowing hard. "I promised I'd talk about it, but I'm afraid you won't like me much after we do."

"That's not possible."

"It has to do with Lara—with why she died. We'd been dating for most of high school. In our senior year, we started fighting about the future. She wanted to go to Harvard, even though she'd been accepted to Stanford as well, and I was trying to change her mind. I was jealous of the mere idea of her being without me. The fight on graduation day was the worst of all. She took off in the car her parents gave her as a graduation present. She never showed up at the graduation ceremony."

He takes a deep breath and I clasp my palms to fists, my nails cutting into the flesh, because I think I know what will follow.

"The police found her a few hours later. She had crashed into a tree with the car."

I jerk up straight, covering my mouth with both hands. "That wasn't your fault, James," I whisper through my fingers.

"Wasn't it? If we hadn't fought before..."

"Many teens lose control of their car."

"She was so upset when she left," he murmurs. I

can hear the guilt in his voice, and I hug him tight. I know how he feels, because I feel guilty too every time I think about Kate, convinced that I could have done more to save her.

"It was not your fault, James. People fight all the time. They get angry all the time."

He kisses my temple, returning my hug. "You're not going to judge me even a little?"

"No, I won't. And you shouldn't judge yourself cither. Or say nonsense, like not being good enough for me."

"I haven't even tried to have a relationship afterward, just meaningless hook-ups. I was afraid I'll hurt someone else... lose someone else. I'm bound to screw up with you."

"We'll fix it. I promise."

He cups my jaw in his hand, kissing me with passion. I kiss him right back, moving my hands all over his arms. When he climbs over me, I wrap my legs around him on instinct. He grinds against me, and fuck, the friction of his cock against me is thrilling, even if we're both wearing clothes.

On a groan, he mutters, "Let's move to your room."

I nod and then he lifts me up. I wrap my legs around him tighter.

"Don't walk to walk to your room?"

"Nope. I'll just cling to you. So many

possibilities to feel you up." I touch his shoulder blades shamelessly to prove my point. He pays me back by fondling my ass, pressing his cock against my belly. Oh, yeah. Tons of possibilities.

He kisses me all the way to my room, then puts me on the bed on my back, taking off my clothes one by one, then his.

I pout. "Let me remove your clothes."

"No. I'll lose control if you touch me, and I want to take my time to savor you."

He spreads my thighs wide, kissing the soft skin on the inside, while his hands travel all over my body. I feel myself getting wet, and when he traces his finger from my entrance up to my clit, I roll my hips, silently begging for more.

James smiles wolfishly, moving to take one of my nipples between his lips. Then he bites gently, and I cry out softly.

"Oh, you have to be silent, Serena." He whispers the words against my sensitive nipple.

"Then you have to stop doing that."

"I won't stop. I'll make you come very hard tonight, I promise."

He moves lower, kissing my torso, then my pubis. He stops at my clit, tracing a circle *around it* with the tip of his tongue. I find the shirt he discarded next to me and bite into it, hoping that the fabric will stifle my moans. This man will drive me insane with pleasure. He circles around my clit until I feel like I'm about to come out of my skin, and then he sucks it into his mouth. I come the next second, crying my pleasure into the pillow.

"Fuck, you're gorgeous all hot like this."

"In me, please. I want you inside me."

"I'm not done eating you out, Serena. I will make you come at least once more before fucking you."

My inner muscles clench at his words. How can dirty talking turn me on so much? James pulls my labia in his mouth, then moves to torture my clit again, while sliding two fingers inside me.

"You're so wet, sweetheart," he says, working me with his fingers. I come again so fast, that I'm embarrassed. I can barely breathe, let alone think, but I'm satisfied that James finally seems to have lost control. He slides on a condom, then pushes inside me, burying himself to the hilt.

I groan, but the shirt masks the sound. James takes it out of my mouth, giving me a soft kiss. "This won't do. I want to kiss you while we're connected like this."

Everything inside me stills as I look into those gorgeous blue eyes. I feel a little raw from his confession, from the beautiful way in which he opened up to me. I can imagine he feels even more vulnerable. I'm going to give him everything he needs tonight. I want to be all he needs forever.

James kisses me the entire time he loves me. He drives inside me without restraint, fucking me deliciously hard, like he can't get enough of me. I plant my heels firmly in the mattress for leverage, and push my hips up with equal desperation. My hands are all over his back, then on the steely muscles of his ass.

When I'm close to yet another climax, James rolls us over, so I'm on top of him.

"Ride me, baby. I want to see you take control of your pleasure."

I feel a little insecure at first, but under his heated gaze, I start to feel bold, moving up and down. His cock rubs me in different spots, depending if I sit up straight or I lean over him to kiss his chest, or his mouth. I'm shaking with pleasure, almost afraid of my orgasm. I want to move faster, but can't find my rhythm.

"James, I need this faster, harder."

He obliges, placing his hands on my hips and lifting me a little. Then he pounds inside me from below, and I think I might faint. He fills me so deeply that I might just dissolve from pleasure. My clit collides with his pubic bone on every thrust, and *my God*, that spot he touches inside me is just exquisite. His cock widens inside me as he starts coming. I didn't think I could feel fuller, but here he is, stretching my pussy, filling me even more.

"Give me your mouth, Serena," he commands, and I lean over him in a kiss as we both climax.

CHAPTER THIRTEEN

James spends almost every other night at my apartment over the next following weeks. Thank God for that, because otherwise, my life becomes a little chaotic.

Two developments took care of that.

One: I was offered three interviews. Two of them were at banks in San Francisco last week. One was at a bank in New York yesterday.

Two: I lost the part-time bookkeeping job I've had since starting college—my only source of income until graduation—because my boss unexpectedly closed down the company, so I started hunting for another job to support myself until I graduate and start a real job.

The day I return from my interview in New York, I'm excited to discover a new email from one of my computer science professors. In my desperation to find any kind of student job, I made use of my computer science minor for the first time ever. One of my professors mentioned in a class that he needed a student to help him on a project, and I jumped at the opportunity. He tells me in this email that I am to come to his office on Friday so he can give me more details and I can start working right away. Excellent.

When I open the door to our apartment, I find Jess crouched over her laptop, her bandaged leg up on the couch, her messy hair bundled up in a bun.

She looks up at me with concern. "You look terrible. Your interview didn't go too well?"

"My interview went fine. I'm just tired. I think I'll sleep for a bit, so I'm not a zombie when James comes to dinner tonight."

She presses her lips together. "You didn't invite Parker as well, did you?"

"Did something happen with Parker?"

She sets her laptop aside and puts her hands together in her lap, watching me like she did when we were in high school when she was about to tell me that she wanted to skip a class and I had to cover up for her.

"He's a jerk, Serena. I don't know how you can stand him."

"I'm sorry, have you *met* Parker? He's nothing

but kind and polite."

"To you maybe," she splutters. "To me he's a prick."

I stare at her, wondering whether her accident has caused some serious brain damage.

He's been around our place quite a few times since Jess got out of the hospital, helping with one thing or another. I think he feels guilty for not preventing Jess's accident, since he was in the bar when it happened. They had a fall out a couple of days ago, I think, but I didn't know it was this serious.

"Want to tell me what's wrong?" I ask gently.

"No, I don't want to talk about it."

I drop the topic and go straight to my bedroom, inspecting my calendar. It's the second week of April now. Fingers crossed that I get a job offer before graduation.

Later that evening, I get an excellent surprise in my inbox. One of the banks in San Francisco offered me a job. I'm jumping up and down, hugging the living lights out of Jess. We can't celebrate with a night of clubbing, because her leg is still in a cast, but I assure her we'll go out as soon as it comes off.

When James arrives at dinner, I hug him too.

"Congratulations, beautiful. I knew you aced that interview."

I rise on my tiptoes, planting my lips on his. "Thank you."

As I set the table for dinner, he asks carefully, "Are you going to accept it?"

"I think so, even though I'd like to hear what the other banks have to say too."

He nods, but his expression clouds. Before I have the chance to ask him about it, he says, "I want us to do something together next weekend. Just the two of us. Go somewhere and relax."

Oh, crap. I feel myself getting smaller. My chest becomes tight.

"Serena, what's wrong?"

"It's just that…it's the anniversary of Kate's death next Saturday, and I'm a bit of a wreck during that time. I wouldn't be much fun."

James immediately comes to me, gently laying his hands at the sides of my face. "All the more reason to go away. I'll distract you, sweetheart."

I lick my lips, unsure what to make of this. On one hand, I love that he's so attentive. But I'm afraid to show him that vulnerable side of me. What if he doesn't like it? Michael wasn't very understanding. He kept saying that enough time has passed, and I should get over it.

"You're overthinking everything," he whispers.

"How do you know?"

"I just do. Relax, Serena. Let me be there for you next weekend. That's all I ask."

"Okay. What do you have in mind?"

"I don't know yet. But I promise it'll be worth the trip."

He pulls me in his arms, and I melt against his strong muscles. God, he's becoming so important to me that I can barely believe it. I find myself hoping there is a future for us, because when I'm with him, everything feels right in the world.

CHAPTER FOURTEEN

On Saturday, I run around in the apartment like crazy, preparing for my trip with James. He's taking me to a very swanky hotel, and as such, I need swanky dinner dresses and shoes.

Music blares loudly through our speakers, and I head to Jess, who is in the kitchen.

"Jess, the neighbors will call the police," I cry. To no avail. She's standing in front of the oven, her back turned to me. With one hand, she's propping herself on her crutch, with the other, she's holding a pan. Her black shorts bear traces of white powder. I instantly recognize the sweet smell floating in the air, filling the entire apartment. Pancakes with caramel topping. Her hair is up in a loose ponytail that looks like it might come down any second now. I walk over to her iPod and turn the volume down a bit.

"Serena," Jess exclaims, jumping so violently that her pancake lands on the floor, spreading grease and powder on our immaculate tiles. "I didn't hear you."

"No wonder," I bend and clean the mess, then wash my hands. "Can I taste one?" I point to the stack of heart-shaped pancakes on the counter.

"Sure, I'll just finish cooking these two. You can eat them all; I was starving and ate three while cooking."

"Excellent," I say. I can never turn down Jess's pancakes. "You're cheerful."

"I'm celebrating tonight."

"What are you celebrating? And how—" I splutter, gesturing at her leg.

"This, my friend, is no reason not to celebrate." She grins. "It's just the perfect excuse so professors aren't that strict with my attendance."

I must admit I never thought she'd get away with this for so long. She's at least half an hour late every day for her classes, but so far, so good. Then again, Jess never needed much besides her smile and maybe a low-cut neckline to talk her way out of anything. A bandaged leg really is the supreme weapon for a skilled persuader like her.

"Besides, I've got real reasons to celebrate. My doctor said he can take the cast off a week earlier." She grins. "I already called the museum in London and they scheduled my interview. I'm flying to London in one month."

"This is wonderful news, Jess."

I'm about to grab another pancake when Jess says, "Can you please bring me another hair band?" She points at her loose ponytail. "This one's about to break and I don't want my hair all over the kitchen."

"Sure."

I pinch my nose when I enter her room. Jess has been smoking inside here more than usual. I find a gray hair band on her desk, and am about to go back in the kitchen, when something on her desk catches my attention. Her vision board lies on the desk—a collection of photographs glued on a cardboard depicting her goals. I recognize the Tower of London in one of the photos.

"Are you ready for your trip?" she asks when I get back.

"Yep. But I'm nervous like hell."

"Because you know I'm a bit depressed on Kate's anniversaries, and I know James said he wants to be by my side, but I'm not sure he understands how much of a mess I can be."

"Well, I think he does. He's not like Michael, you know."

"I know."

"That idiot made you feel like it was wrong to

be sad about your sister. From what you've told me, James understands about loss."

I hadn't considered that, but she is right. A weight lifts off my shoulders, though I'm still not entirely at ease.

When James picks me up, one hour later, I try to push my worries at the back of my mind. We make small talk, and he doesn't push me to talk, but from time to time, he just touches my hand, squeezing it reassuringly.

About three hours later, we arrive at our destination. The hotel is at the edge of one of California's redwood forests, and the sight of the giant sequoia trees takes my breath away.

When our hotel comes into view, I'm giddy with excitement. It used to be a mansion, and now it's a luxury hotel.

I take a full minute when I'm inside to admire the decor: the cherry wood furniture, the intricately painted high ceiling, and the centerpiece of the room—the beautiful chandelier.

Our room is even more beautiful, with a huge window that overlooks the forrest of giant sequoias. Because we left after lunch, it's already dinnertime, so James and I dress up, then head to the restaurant.

The restaurant is as impressive as the reception

area. The furniture is made of the same cherry wood, and the high ceiling is also painted—albeit in different patterns. The biggest difference is that instead of one enormous chandelier, there are a lot of smaller ones hanging from the ceiling here and there. It looks cozier this way, even though it's still luxurious enough that I'm a bit intimidated as James and I sit in a corner where there are no other patrons.

"This place is beautiful, James."

"I thought you'd like it."

The waiter gives each of us a menu, and I flip through the pages with interminable lists of wines for a few minutes before putting it down.

"Why don't you order wine for both of us?"

"What would you say if we start with champagne? After all, we have things to celebrate."

"Sounds good."

He orders a bottle of champagne I've never heard of, and the waiter brings it almost immediately.

"To you, Serena," he says, holding the glass up.

My cheeks flame. "To us."

We clink glasses, and then I take the first sip. "This is delicious."

"Why do you sound so surprised?"

"I'm usually not a champagne girl, but this is great."

His phone buzzes, but he mutes it. It happened quite a few times on the trip here as well.

"Why won't you take that?"

"It's Natalie. She's been trying to get in contact with me, but I've been ignoring her."

"Why?"

"Let's just say we're not in a very good place. I had an opportunity to buy her shares, and I did it. I forced her out of the company."

"What? Why?"

"Because it was time."

"You're being very cryptic."

"Natalie was trying to use her shares to manipulate me."

"She wanted you, didn't she?"

"Yes. Frankly, she'd been causing trouble for a long time, even though she had to know we'd never work out. She has a tendency to… not let me forget the past." His neck stiffens. "I don't think she does it on purpose. We just seem to bring out the worst in each other."

"But you were with her. She said something like that at your parents' party."

"Years ago, yes. I was in a bad place, and she didn't seem to mind."

"But why now?"

"Because she made it clear that she didn't like you, and that she'd cause trouble. I don't want that kind of drama for us."

Wow. Wow. Wow.

"James, that's…I don't know what to say." I'm humbled.

"You don't have to say anything. It's something I should have done a long time ago, but having you in my life made me realize it was time to let go of toxic people. Let's focus on our celebration."

I don't pay attention to how many glasses I'm drinking until I realize that I'm tipsy.

"Whoops," I exclaim, accidentally stabbing my plate instead of a fry.

"Serena?" James asks with amusement. "Are you drunk?"

"No," I protest. "I mean…I don't know. Am I?"

"You've had a few glasses."

I pout. "This is all your fault."

"Is it now?"

"Yep. Even though now you appear even sexier, so I'm not too sure I'm mad."

"So without alcohol I'm not sexy?" he asks on a grin.

"Not what I said, but now my thoughts are shameless. I'm imagining exactly what will happen in our room, how I will trace all those muscles with my tongue. Yumm."

"Serena, stop with that line of conversation. It's

turning me on."

I clap my hands. "Precisely what I want. Told you this is your fault. Now you have to pay. Why didn't you stop me?"

He leans forward, whispering conspiratorially, "Who knows what I can persuade you to do if you're tipsy."

"You fiendish man. Are you saying I'm not sexually adventurous enough for you?"

"Oh, you are." He swallows hard, looking around. "Let's change the subject."

"Why, you're afraid you'll lose control?" I tease. "If I talk about sex? If I say I can't wait to have you inside me?"

"Serena," he says warningly.

"Well, it's true. I also can't wait to get on my knees, and—"

"That's it, woman. I'm taking you to our room."

I lean back in the chair, faking disinterest. "Nope. I think I'll hang around here for a little while longer, tease the hell out of you."

"You do that, and the other patrons are in for a show."

"Oh, please. You have no leverage. All you can do here is kiss me."

He smiles like a little devil. "Exactly. And I can kiss you until you moan."

Well…heck. The man has a point. He's a great

kisser.

"Okay. Let's go to the room."

"You're giving in so fast?"

"You're promising kisses."

"I am."

The second I get up from my chair, I realize that wherever the room is, it can't be close enough. I gulp and clutch my tiny envelope bag tightly to my chest. The spinning only gets worse when I start walking. James sustains me as I walk.

"Wow, this is worse than I thought," I murmur.

"I've got you, sweetheart," he says and swipes me right off my feet.

"James, no," I half-cry, half-laugh, clinging to him, praying not to throw up. James's chest reverberates with laughter. He's got one arm around my back and the other one under my knees. I keep my eyes closed the entire time, taking in deep breaths. The scent of his ocean and musk cologne travels down my throat, exciting and calming me at the same time.

"Right, I have to put you down, or I won't be able to unlock the door," he says when we arrive.

He lays me on the black four-poster bed with creamy, transparent curtains around it.

"My head is spinning. Ugh…James…I don't think I'm up for sexy fun."

“That’s okay. I can just hold you.” He climbs in bed next to me, pulling me to him until my head rests on his chest. “How are you holding up, Serena?”

I know he’s referring to Kate.

"Would you rather talk about it or forget about it?" James asks.

"I don't know," I say truthfully. "This is her birthday too, not just the anniversary of her death. When we were kids, we used to have fun on her birthday, before the drugs came.”

"What did you do on her birthdays?"

"Oh, nothing fancy. Usually my mum would prepare a roast chicken and bake a cake in the evening. Before dinner, Kate and I would get up on the roof of our home and release a helium balloon, and watch it soar up in the sky until Mum would call to us that dinner was ready." My mother's voice rings in my head as if she were calling to me right now, *Catherine, Serena, get down here girls before your father eats the chicken all by himself.*

"A balloon? Why?"

"I don't really remember why; I just know we always did it. It's one of the earliest memories I have of us together."

I was six, dressed in a bubble-gum-pink dress, the same color of the balloon we released that day. Kate had the brilliant idea to test whether she could fly with the balloon and almost slipped off the roof. *Shh, don't tell Mum*, Kate said, all giddy and breathing heavily.

A familiar emptiness inside my chest starts creeping in, but it hurts less than it usually does, and I'm not sure why.

"You've got such a lovely smile," James says.

I turn my head slightly in his direction. "I… I was just replaying a memory in my head. I'm getting sleepy."

"Don't fight it. I'll just be here, holding you."

As he kisses my forehead in one soft brush, putting an arm around me, I know why I'm not hurting so much, why I remember sweet moments. Bccause James is with me, holding me in a way I've never been held. Tears appear in the corners of my eyes, and I let them fall, one by one, until I drift off to sleep.

CHAPTER FIFTEEN

I wake up covered with something soft and warm up to the tip of my nose. James put a blanket on me. But he's not in bed. Hmmm…where could he have gone? It's dark outside. I feel much better, and I realize the air in the room is fresh. James opened the door to the terrace.

I take in a mouthful of air, pondering for a few moments what woke me up, when I hear the call.

"Serena." It's James's voice.

I spring to my feet, wobbling a little on my sandals, and looking to my left and right.

"Where are you?" I call, grinning.

"I'll wait for you to figure it out," James says, and I can tell by the way he sounds that he, too, is grinning. "It's more fun."

The sound doesn't come from the bedroom, but inexplicably, from the edge of the terrace, so I put on some shoes and walk toward there and bend over the railing. Sure enough, James stands on the ground, leaning with one shoulder against the wall and beaming up at me.

"You sleep like a rock. I've been calling out for at least ten minutes," he says.

"What on earth are you doing down there?"

"Pondering whether I should bring a ladder or…"

I gasp. "You want me to jump down there?"

He grins, unhitching himself from the wall, hands in pockets. "Correct."

"You've got to be kidding, right?"

"Come on. It's not that high."

Truth be told, it isn't that high. But I've never been much of a climber, or jumper for that matter.

"Whatever happened to just walking down some stairs like a normal person? There must be other ways to get there. "

"I picked the least boring one." James winks, holding his arms up. "I thought you'd find it romantic."

"It kind of is," I admit with a giggle. Unless I break a leg, or my neck. I bite the inside of my cheek, eyeing the wooden railing for a few seconds, then swing a leg over the railing, careful not to damage my pink dress in the process. The edge of the terrace on the other side of the railing is just wide enough for me to stand on my toes. I bend my knees, holding onto the railing as best as I can. The ground really isn't that far away. I could almost touch James's raised arms if I extended one of my own. But the sinking feeling in my stomach refuses to let go.

"You'll have to actually let go of the railing to be able to jump, Serena," James jokes.

"You don't say."

I slowly release my right hand from the railing, holding tight with the left one.

"That's it," James says, touching the tip of my fingers. "Jump, baby. I'll catch you."

Gritting my teeth, I let go of the railing completely, and lean forward.

"Aargh," I yelp, as I crash into James's arms, almost knocking him over. My feet land with a thump on the ground. The heels of my sandals have sunk almost an inch into the soft earth. "My shoes are so not right for this," I say.

James laughs softly in my ear, his arms wrapped around me. My heartbeat picks up. "That's a cheap way of tricking me into carrying you."

"I swear I wasn't—" the rest of my words come out in a howl as he lifts me in his arms again, like earlier when he took me to my room.

"Better?"

"I can get used to this, you know."

"Good," he says, looking me straight in the eyes. "That's what I want. No actually, I want more. I don't want you to only get used to me. I want you to be addicted to me, like I am to you."

"I already am addicted to you, James. Where are you taking me?"

"You don't think I'd tell you, do you?"

He climbs a slope, and I take in the giant sequoia trees around us. He carries me until

the trees become scarcer and I see a clearing not far in front of us. There is light in the clearing, which is odd, given that it's in the heart of the forest. When we get closer, I narrow my eyes, staring at the lighting device—a huge *thing* on the ground, like a giant turtle whose grotesquely deformed shell…as if it's made of fluorescent ostrich eggs.

But as we step inside the clearing, I get to see what it really is. It's not a lighting device at all. It's a stack of white balloons tied to a stone on the ground. They are somehow lit up on the inside. Next to them is a picnic blanket.

Balloons. Eight of them. One for each one of Kate's anniversaries since she died.

My throat is dry as James kneels and puts me on the blanket, next to the balloons. My tear ducts, on the other hand, aren't. James sits by me, on the blanket.

"How come they're glowing?" I ask, fighting very hard to keep my voice from shaking.

"They've got LEDs in them." He interlaces his fingers with mine. "I thought it'd be good for you to do this again."

I tilt my head to the side, wiping a tear away with my other hand. "When did you do... all this?"

"After you fell asleep. I was afraid you'd wake up before I returned, but the champagne knocked you out all right," he chuckles, squeezing my fingers gently.

"What time is it?"

"Two o'clock."

So it's her birthday already.

I reach out to the balloons, barely touching them. I don't know why James thinks it would be good for me to release them up into the sky. Seeing them already brings the familiar suffocating lump in my chest. But I start untying one of the balloons, with trembling hands, if only to get rid of them, so I don't have to keep looking at them.

The moment I untie it, the balloon soars up. I untie two more before James says, "Don't let them go all at once. Take your time." He's propped on his elbows on the blanket, staring up at the sky. He motions to me to lie next to him. I hesitate, looking from him to the remaining balloons in the stack, then lie back on my elbows too.

I look up at the black sky, and I grit my teeth at the sight of the three glowing bulbs. From here, it looks like fire burns inside them. Bright and inextinguishable. Yet, as I watch them go higher and higher, something happens to the lump in my chest.

Something I wasn't expecting.

It eases. Slowly, very slowly, as if someone were pulling it out bit by bit with a clipper. The balloons become so small they could almost pass for stars, if they weren't moving upward. Eventually, they get lost in the clouds and I don't see them anymore.

I untie another one, and watch it sail up in the sky after the others, farther and farther away, taking my pain with it.

"It looks a bit like a star." I only realize I said it out loud when James chuckles. My cheeks heat up instantly. He'll think I'm five years old.

"You're right, it does."

"People say to make a wish when you see a falling star. Do you think it will work if I make one now?"

"I think there is no such thing as a bad time to make a wish," he says softly.

The balloon is so high now, I almost can't see it anymore, and an irrational panic grips me. I have to spell my wish out before it disappears in the clouds. I have to. Maybe it can carry my wish to her.

I wish Kate could forgive me for not doing more for her.

And maybe my guilt floats in the air like a damned aura, or maybe he can just read it off me, but James says, "Don't blame yourself."

I turn my head to the right until I can't see him even from the corner of my eye. "I can’t help it." I focus my gaze on a tree in the distance.

"People sometimes make bad choices, Serena. Kate made quite a few. Trust me, no matter how much you try to deter them, they will still make them. Even when they know just how bad those choices are for them. Mostly they do it because they think those bad choices are the only thing they deserve."

There is a long pause, and when he speaks again, his voice sounds dead. "The worst choices are the ones who hurt others. And I made enough of those myself."

I turn around, and find him gazing at the sky, his eyes glassy with tears.

Of course, that's why he sensed my guilt. He knows the feeling only too well. "James, that's not—"

"Do you want to release the rest of the balloons?" he interrupts, sitting up straight. "You've got four left." He presses his palms on his eyes briefly, then plasters a fake smile on his face.

I sit up straight too. "No, I want you to release them. For Lara."

The smile freezes on his face. "I don't think this is such a good idea."

"Just try it," I say, untying a balloon and shoving it into his hand. "For me."

"You're not playing fair," he whispers, his eyes begging.

"Please."

He tilts his head, staring down at the balloon in his hand. He lets go of it, following it with his gaze. I don't watch the balloon at all. Instead, I watch him. The muscles around his eyes and mouth tighten; his fingers dig deep in the blanket.

"Let's release the rest together," he murmurs after a while. We take the balloons together, and release them.

After what seems like an eternity, he turns to me.

"Smile for me," he says and relief surges through me. His features melt into a heartfelt smile too, his eyes brimming with warmth.

"One smile from you can make everything

better. This is all I'll ever need."

At this moment, I truly believe we can mend each other. More than that, I almost think we can complete each other. I know he can complete me.

My heart throbs against my ribcage as I put one palm on his chest and then the other, not quite meeting his eyes, gazing at the top button of his shirt instead. His heart drums under my fingers, with a lightning-quick rhythm that matches my own.

I bite my lip and close my eyes, seeking his lips.

They're smooth and warm and waiting for me. They are slightly open. Inviting. I take my time to enjoy them, my eyes still closed. I kiss the upper lip first, pulling at it slightly with my teeth. He groans against my mouth, making the skin on my entire body tingle. I move to his lower lip, and when I finish torturing it, when I finally kiss him—he touches me, putting one palm on the small of my back. When we pause for breath, he murmurs,

"Are you sure about this, Serena?"

"I'm trembling like a leaf; I'd say I'm pretty damn sure," I joke, my voice weak.

James bites his lip, his other hand tucking a strand of hair behind my ear. His hand is shaking. "We can wait until tomorrow."

"I don't want to awit."

When our lips meet again, he completely loses it. His hand presses my back, flattening me against him as his mouth covers mine in a rough move, his tongue seeking mine in a desperate dance. I gasp for breath when his lips leave my mouth, descending down my neck, marking a trail of flames on their way to my breasts.

"Make love to me, James," I beg, frantically undoing the buttons of his shirt, then tossing the black fabric in the grass. The sight of his naked torso cuts my breath short. He opens the zipper of my dress, and in one, gratifying second, his hands abrade my back, his nails digging in my skin. I get stuck on the button of his pants, as usual. With one soft laugh, James removes his pants altogether. I let my dress fall. James swallows hard when it slides down my shoulders. I'm not wearing a bra. I kick my dress away as he cups my breasts, my eyes latched onto his. I sit down on the blanket, then lie on my back, pulling him on top of me.

"I want to get lost in you," I say. His arms lie by my sides, his warm body shielding me from the chilling night breeze.

James smiles against my lips, "I want to get lost in us."

Lost in us. I could do that.

I smile too. We both have goose bumps all over

our bodies.

James's hand slides to my hip, and then to my panties—the only piece of fabric I still have on. I mirror his movement, my hand pulling at the waistband of his boxers, and then… *God.* Desire slams through me as I palm his erection. Hot and huge. He chokes on his next breath, and in one swift move, removes my panties.

No. He didn't just remove them. He ripped them apart. His hot, heavy breaths send shivers through me, as his tongue nuzzles at my nipple, while his fingers stroke my folds, slow and teasing.

I moan deeply when they touch my clit, arching my back.

"James," I gasp, digging my nails in his arms, trying to pull him up, so I can kiss him. I need more of this. More of him.

He rises abruptly, then urges my knees apart, spreading my legs. Fisting my hair, he pulls me into a fierce kiss.

And then he thrusts inside me. Raw and hard and filling. There is nothing between us, because we stopped using condoms last week, since I'm on the pill.

I moan in his mouth, his own groan reverberating across his chest. I press my hips to him, and then the back and forth dance begins. He keeps his moves deliberately slow, spreading relief and desire through every nerve, making my toes curl and my insides scream. I grab his backside with both hands, pushing him harder against me, opening my legs wider. He groans against my shoulder, biting me, his nails digging in my thigh. The clamping of our hips becomes faster. More urgent. The moans blow up into screams and roars, the woods around us amplifying the sounds. My breath catches as I feel the orgasm starting to build inside me.

It starts as a pulsation deep inside me—at my most intimate spot, but the electric jolts travel to every corner, every cell of my body.

"Please," I beg, burying my head in his neck, my cheek caressing his moist skin. The sweet smell of sweat on his neck sends me over the edge.

"Serena, God," he cries, arching back his neck, plunging inside me with a brutality I welcome. I grab the blanket with both fists, pulling at it with all my might as relief consumes me.

CHAPTER SIXTEEN

I swear loudly when I open my eyes next morning.

"Good morning to you too, sailor," James shouts.

"Will you keep your voice down?" I bury my head under the pillow. "I've got the most horrible migraine."

"It's called a hangover around here. And it won't get better if you hide under the sheets. Come on, it's past noon."

"Great," I mumble, throwing the pillow away, and forcing myself in a sitting position. I pull the sheets all around me, because I am completely naked. James stands, leaning on one of the bedposts, dressed in shorts and nothing else, staring at me. And even though the creamy, transparent curtain obscures him somewhat, I can see that he looks wide awake. Beautiful. Stunning. I, on the other hand, feel like a bulldozer ran over me. I bet I look exactly like that, too. It was early morning when we returned to the room after watching the sunset.

"Can you pass me the backpack?" I ask. He doesn't budge, folding his arms on his chest, observing me with a smile. "What?"

"Nothing."

He unhitches himself from the bedpost and walks toward the glass doors where the backpack is. I steal a glance at myself in the oval mirror and swear again—this time not out loud. My mascara is smeared all around my eyes; my hair is a downright mess, sticking out in every direction. I try desperately to tame it, running my fingers through it, but this only seems to make it worse. I look like an electrocuted raccoon. Suddenly, I remember Jess's theory about the "kiss of the witch": the magical process through which a girl wakes up in the morning, only to find herself looking like a witch instead of the princess she was when she went to bed. The chances of this happening increase exponentially, the hotter the guy next to her is. It must be avoided at all cost for the guy to see her like this, either by waking up before him and sneaking in the bathroom to freshen up, or by keeping emergency toiletries and a makeup bag under the bed. Otherwise, the guy will bolt faster than a witch on a broomstick.

Since I have no such emergency bag, I weigh my chances of sneaking to the bathroom without James realizing. As he tosses the backpack in front of me, sitting on the edge of the bed, my chances plummet somewhere below zero. So I keep my head bent so he can't see my eyes, searching in the backpack.

I find my phone charger in the backpack, along with some books for the courses I'll have on Monday.

"Why are you keeping your head bent like that?" James asks.

"Umm…"I bite my lip. "I'm just searching for something in here."

His fingers slide under my chin, lifting my head.

"I don't want you to see me looking like a raccoon," I admit.

He bursts out laughing, guffaw after guffaw bubbling out of his chest. "Why? You're the loveliest raccoon I've come across."

"Don't mock me."

"I'm not," he says, suddenly serious. "I like to watch you wake up. I…" Inching closer to me, his fingers trail up and down on my cheek.

A knock at the door breaks the moment. "Room service," a man's voice calls from behind the door.

"I'll handle that," James says, standing up. He

takes my hand and kisses the back of it, watching me longingly. Heat spreads through me, making my head feel bubbly.

The second James opens the door, I seize my chance, grab the backpack, and slip inside the bathroom.

I reemerge from it half an hour later. I don't quite look like a princess, but I no longer look like a witch, either. I had to seriously rub my face to get the mascara off, but now it's one hundred percent gone. My black hair is clean and tamed, hanging around my shoulders in loose waves. I'm wearing a short green dress with a black belt and flip-flops. The room is empty, a smell of bacon and coffee lingering in the air. I plug in my phone and follow the smell outside on the terrace.

The sun shines brightly above us, inundating the terrace, in the center of which a table and two chairs appeared. James is now slightly more dressed, wearing a white T-shirt and his boxers.

"Oh my God, did you order the entire menu?" I ask, ogling at the ten or so platters on the table. It's only then that I realize James is talking on the phone. It's not a pleasant conversation either, because he's frowning, his palm rolled in a fist.

"We are not having this conversation again, Dani," he says, as I sit opposite him, and I can tell he's making an inhumane effort not to shout at her. Dani, on the other hand, isn't making any effort. I can hear her shouts from where I'm seated. I pretend not to hear anything, serving myself coffee, bacon, scrambled eggs, and toast. I'll try the five types of fish and almost as many jams later on.

"Fine, I'll talk to you later," he snaps, closing his phone.

"How is Dani?" I ask, smearing butter on my toast.

"She's starting to channel me when I was her age." His voice is trembling with anger. "I have no idea what's gotten into her. It all started with her wanting to go to parties more often, and now she's… I'm terrified of her going all alone to England."

"What do your parents say?"

"My mom lives on her own planet, and my dad won't realize something's off unless she busts her trust fund, like I did." He stabs a piece of bacon with his fork so forcefully that the metal pierces through it, scratching the plate underneath with an ear-splitting sound. "I don't want to talk about Dani anymore."

"All right. So, tell me, what are we doing today? We're exploring the forest, right?"

"That's why we're here. And after we're done with that, I can explore you."

"Of course. How could I forget that?" I tease. "But the forest is my priority. I've wanted to see it for a long time."

"Why didn't you?"

"Michael wasn't keen on the idea."

"Right," he says. "Have you heard from him since you broke up?"

"No." I take one of his hands in mine, interlacing my fingers between his clenched ones. "Don't be jealous of him, James. He's nothing to me. Nothing."

"Of course I'm jealous of him," he says, though the tension in his fingers loosens a tad. "The guy had you for six years. He must have done something right"

"You've made me feel more alive in the time I've spent with you than he did in six years."

"Is that so?" He comes next to me, hooking an arm around my waist and pulling me against him in a fraction of a second.

We lock eyes, and all words escape me as I stare into his deep blue eyes. I wish there was a way I could let him know just how alive he makes me feel. How he turns the blood in my veins to liquid fire.

"Serena, I'd like you to consider something. I know it's a huge request, and we've only known each other for two months, but I'd like you to consider it."

"Okay," I say carefully.

"I know you're still waiting for the answer from the bank in New York, but if I get a vote, I'd really love it if you stayed in San Francisco. This thing between us, I'm afraid we'll lose it if you move away."

He looks straight at me, and the vulnerability in his eyes humbles me.

"Of course you get a vote. I don't even want to move to New York. I just applied there because I was desperate. It means a lot to me that you're saying this to me."

He smiles, kissing my forehead. "It means a lot to me that you're taking my wish into account." We stay like that, entangled in each other, for a while, before he says, "Let's start exploring the forest, woman. Because then I want to come back and make love to you for two days straight."

CHAPTER SEVENTEEN

One month later, I drive Jess to the airport with the windows rolled down, because the AC in her archaic Prius has stopped working, and this is an unusually hot mid-May evening. Jess sits with her hands in her lap, her fingers fiddling with her black cotton skirt. She wears a white simple shirt with the flag of England on it. She drew it herself on the shirt, identical to the one she had drawn on her cast, which her doctor removed a while ago. From time to time, I see her hand sliding to her knee, pinching the skin as if she still can't quite believe her leg is freed up from all the bandages. But her newly found freedom isn't why she's been silent the whole trip, biting her lip as if she's determined to wreck it. For the first time ever, Jess is nervous. Her flight to London is in a couple of hours, her interview tomorrow.

"You'll do fine, Jess."

"I hope so. Sorry I made you drive me to the

airport. I know you're trying to save your evenings for James."

"It's alright," I assure her. "Though he'll probably be asleep by the time I arrive at his place."

The last month has been extraordinary. James and I have been inseparable. Or well. . .as inseparable as it gets. Between our crazy schedules, we only have time for each other in the evening. We spend every night together, either at my place or at his (mostly his). Just thinking about him fills me with bliss.

I drop Jess at the airport, and she promises to call me as soon as she arrives in England.

When I arrive at his place, James is asleep. I slide next to him in the bed, but for some reason, I can't sleep. Exhausted as I am, a strange energy, emanating from deep inside my chest, fills up every cell in my body. I wonder if it's possible to be *too* happy. I prop myself on an elbow, watching him in the dim light coming from the lamp on his nightstand. He sleeps on his stomach, with his back exposed. I trail my fingers on his lips, aching to feel them on mine again. I can't help myself and steal a quick kiss.

His eyes blink open.

"I'm sorry, I didn't want to wake you up."

"What time is it?" he mumbles.

"It's late. Go back to sleep."

"Not a chance," he says. We are both naked. His arm curves around my waist, and he pulls me so close to him, I can feel his erection against my leg. Every nerve in my body becomes hyper-aware of the closeness between us. God, I will never have enough of him. I can only hope he'll never have enough of me, either.

"You naughty boy. What were you dreaming about?"

"You," he whispers against my lips.

"And what were you doing to me?"

"Exactly what I'll do now. Turn around," he commands, his eyes implacable. My folds drip with desire. I do as he says, preparing to lift myself on all fours, but he pushes me into the mattress, with my back up, climbing on top of me, the muscles of his torso pressing against my back. He slings an arm under me, cupping my breast. No air reaches my lungs as he twists my nipple gently.

His hot, irregular breaths make the hairs at the nape of my neck stand on end. His other hand touches me right where I need it to.

"Christ, you're wet already." His teeth pull gently at my earlobe. "Who's the naughty one now?"

I open my mouth to answer, but instead of

words, a moan comes out, as he starts circling my clit with his fingers, plunging inside so deep I'm certain I'll fall apart under him. He pulls out, then thrusts again and again, filling me. I can't move under him, arch my back, or escape in any way the pressure of his fingers circling my tender spot. And this makes it so much more intense. My whole body shakes under him as wave after wave of quivers ravage me, cold sweat forming on my skin. It kills me that I can barely touch him. My hands seek his skin desperately. Spasms tear me apart, starting from the spot where his blessed fingers work their magic on me. I search the pillow, biting into it.

"Don't. I want to hear you scream, Serena," he gushes in my ear.

And so I scream, as the sound of his own relief fills my ears.

Silence follows, as he falls on top of me, his ragged breaths chilling me. I don't know how long we stay like this before he moves to the side, pulling me in an embrace. I kiss him softly, then snuggle against his chest. He interlaces his fingers with mine, touching my forehead with his lips.

"I want to spend forever with you," he murmurs.

A wave of warmth spreads through me.

We fall asleep again, but it's still dark when a

screeching sound wakes me up. With a start, I realize it's a phone.

"Must be Jess," I say. I make a fuzzy mental calculation. It's *very* late in the night here. She couldn't have landed.

"It's my phone," James mumbles. I hear him grope for it in the darkness. "Parker's calling." We both bolt upright in the bed. Whatever it is, it can't be good. While James answers, I turn on the light. And freeze. James sits at the edge of the bed, his face contorted in a mask of astonishment as he listens to Parker. "Why didn't you call me until now?" Parker speaks quickly on the other end. "I'm on my way."

"What happened?"

"I'll tell you later, I must leave. Get back to sleep. On second thought, would you mind coming with me to the office? I'll explain everything in the car."

Ten minutes later, we are in the car, speeding to his office.

"James? What's wrong?"

He takes a deep breath. "My programmers have fucked up a part of the code on our online platform."

"Bugs aren't unusual."

"No, but I have a meeting with investors tomorrow," he glances at the clock. It's five a.m.

“Today actually. In the morning. If the code can't be fixed, the platform won't be working, I won't have anything to show to them." He stops, taking in another deep breath. Parker rounded up every programmer we know, and they’ve been there for hours with no result. Maybe we can help.”

“You certainly can. I'm not half as skilled as those brainiacs you know, but I’ll happily try and help."

"You're as skilled as they are, Serena. Don't try to convince me of the opposite."

"How bad will it be if you aren't able to show the platform to the investors tomorrow?"

He laughs nervously. "How bad? I think it's safe to say ramen noodles will become a big part of my diet." I clench my fists. Bankruptcy.

The second the elevator doors open on the floor of James's office, I feel like I've just entered a football stadium. Parker wasn't exaggerating. He really must have called up every single programmer he knows. There are at least six times more people than there should be in this office, and their constant chatter, punctuated by the occasional shout from one side of the room to the other, pierces my ears in an unpleasant way. The air is thick with exhaustion and the smell of too many people, and the heat of too many computers.

“Serena, I’ll go to Parker.” James winks to someone and then I see the person I was least expecting to see here. Walking up to me, every bit as hairless and smug as on the plane, is Ralph. Between the talk of constant partying and Christie's heavy-handed hints that his only occupation was spending his trust fund, he's the last person I expected to find in a room where everyone is working hard. Ralph is watching me with his abnormally bushy eyebrows raised.

“Ralph, show her what needs to be done,” James says, and takes off.

"Come on," Ralph says, and without another word leads the way into the chaos. He seems to know exactly where he's going, because he doesn't hesitate. As we squeeze ourselves between groups of people huddled around computers, I notice Parker, throwing his hands in the air in despair, talking with less grace than I've ever heard him talk. He doesn't see me.

"Right," Ralph says when we reach the corner of the room where there is a desk with three computers and four twenty-something guys seated in front of two of them, staring at the screen. "Everyone, this is Serena." One of them raises his hand and waves without looking in my direction. The others don't acknowledge me at all.

"Sit here." Ralph points to one of the two empty

chairs in front of the third computer. He sits himself next to me and explains in a few hurried sentences what the issue is. To increase the platform's speed, the programmers did some last-minute modifications to the back-end code yesterday after James went home. Somewhere in those modified lines of code lies the bug that caused the platform to completely crash.

"We've been working on finding the bug the entire night, but another pair of eyes is more than welcome."

I gulp, watching Ralph lean forward in his seat. His elbows on the desk, he rests his chin on his right hand, his eyes beginning to scan the lines of code. An entire night is a long time to be looking for a bug without finding it. Especially when there are a few dozen people looking for it. I check my watch. It's five thirty in the morning.

With my heart pounding fast, and without another word, I turn my attention to the screen, too. It takes me some time to get acquainted with the code well enough to actually be able to search for a bug.

The constant chatter around me is distracting, as is the suffocating air. The tension in the air is almost palpable, like the thinnest sheet of fog. I try to block out all of it. I try to think that this is just another course assignment. One that I've delayed until the last moment. Who am I kidding? I never left anything until the last moment. And no assignment ever had stakes like this.

I lean forward, closer to the screen, flexing my wrist. At some point during the last hour, I rested my chin on my wrist, like Ralph. He's now so close to the screen that if he leans in a few inches more he'll touch the screen with the tip of his nose. I focus my eyes on the screen and read the lines of code until my vision is blurry. I squeeze my eyes shut and open them again a few times. My gaze slides at the lower right corner of the computer, at the clock. Another hour passed. I swallow hard.

Ralph's voice makes me jump. "You're not reading anymore; you're just gazing at that screen, that's no good. You need a break. So do I."

I realize he's right. Both my elbows are on the desk, and I've got no memory of putting them there.

Ralph leans back in his chair, massaging his neck. I mirror his movements, and discover that my own neck is stiffer than I thought. Around me, everyone is glued to their computers, some focused, some on the verge of falling asleep. The guys sharing our desks are part of the latter group.

"You looked surprised to see me here," Ralph says and I turn to him. He's smirking.

“I knew that your favorite pastimes include

spending obscene amounts of money on brainless activities."

"They do," Ralph says, not looking the least bit insulted. "But now and then I like to put my hacking skills to some good use. You know, with whatever neurons I haven't killed with brainless activities." Ralph opens his mouth, but instead of another provocation, he simply says, "James."

I jump to my feet and swirl around.

"Has he been holding you back?" James asks me seriously.

"What? No. We've been in front of the computer for two whole hours and nothing."

James tenses up at the word nothing. "Well, we've got two more left, and then it'll be over either way." He's still smiling, but in an ironic way. It gives me chills.

"What do you mean?" I ask, my heart pounding like mad.

"That's the investors' deadline. They're going to pull back all their support and investment if it's not fixed."

"But that's insane."

"I need coffee," Ralph says, rising from his seat. He swings an arm over my shoulders, leaning into me. I bite my tongue to keep myself from grimacing as a pungent stink emanates from his underarm. "Do you think you can convince the boss not to kill me if I go on a coffee break?"

"I need coffee too. I think everyone needs some," I say, not because I want to side with Ralph, but because I genuinely don't think anyone in this room can work two more minutes, let alone two more hours, if they don't get caffeine in their system. I unhitch Ralph's arms from my shoulders. The smell of him nauseates me.

"I know," James says, his fists loose now. "That's why I ordered coffee for everyone."

As if on cue, I hear a *ping* from the other side of the room. The elevator doors open and two women appear, one in her forties and one who doesn't look older than me, pushing coffee carts with plastic cups inside the room. I realize now that I could only hear the *ping* because the chatter in the room has dropped to an almost non-existent level. Two hours ago, I would've given everything for silence, but now I know it's a sign that everyone is truly exhausted.

And so does James.

"Excellent timing," I say, as Ralph darts in the direction of the coffee cart.

James links his gaze to mine. "Smile for me."

The corners of my lips instantly lift into a smile.

He smiles as well, then turns to face the room. "Everyone, coffee is here," James says loudly. "Fill up, and please get back to work. There is just under two hours left and I have full confidence that someone in this room of amazing people will find the bug." The desperation that pierced his voice a few minutes ago isn't there anymore. His voice is energetic, lively. Inspiring even. "And then we can all go celebrate at Wellstone's. My treat."

There are a few appreciative whistles and some applause. Wellstone's is one of the most expensive places around. I head along with every person in the room toward the coffee cart. I wait patiently in the long line that forms in front of it. One glance around the room reveals that not everyone is in the line. James and Parker are seated at their desks, eyes fixed on their computer screens.

When I finally do manage to get my hands on a cup of steamy coffee, I start looking for Ralph. I find him in front of the elevator, an arm swung around the shoulders of a tall woman with red hair. Ralph's holding a cup of coffee in one hand—the one around her shoulders—and a pack of cigarettes in the other one.

"Ralph, I hope you're not thinking of sneaking outside to smoke. There's no time for that."

Ralph turns around in an instant, and the redhead steps away from him, looking relieved. Judging by the youthful roundness of her face and the nervous way she glances around her, as if expecting someone to reprimand her for her behavior, she must be an intern.

"Ana here and I were just going for a quick smoke."

"I am sure you can do that after the deadline," I say. I don't specifically say you and Ana because I'm almost one hundred percent sure that Ana has no desire to go anywhere with Ralph. Sure enough, she smiles apologetically and darts off.

Ralph looks at me grimly then shoves the package in the pocket of his jeans.

"I can smoke a cigarette in under a minute, you know," he grumbles as we head back to our desk.

"I don't care how fast you smoke. The only thing I care about is how fast you can find this damn bug."

We slump in our seats. Staring in his coffee cup, he says, "You honestly believe we'll find it on time?"

I don't answer.

"It's all your fault, you know."

"What?"

"Why do you think the investors are so ruthless?"

"Because that's how investors are."

"They liked Natalie, and James forced her out. That's why they're so eager to pull back their support."

His words are like a punch in the gut. So all of

this is my fault?

Instead of saying anything else, I start looking at the lines of code on the screen again, not taking my eyes off it even as I sip coffee from my cup. The noise of steps and chairs being pulled as everyone returns to work distracts me, and I find myself staring at the clock in the corner of the screen instead of the code. Once everyone has taken their seats, stone silence sets in again. The silence makes it even harder for me to concentrate than the noise. My eyes don't leave the computer screen even for a fraction of a second in the period that follows. They blur again. I try to avoid looking at the clock, but my gaze slides there more often than I'd like. When there's less than an hour left, Ralph props a piece of paper on the lower part of the screen, hiding the clock. I wipe my palms on my legs repeatedly because they're sweaty as hell. Ralph jiggles his foot in a nerve-wracking way, and I put my right hand firmly on his leg when I can't stand it anymore. He stops right away. Somewhere in the room, someone swears again and again in a heavy English accent. Parker.

And then something that might be a squeal or a scream pierces the air and for a second I fear it might actually split my head in two. More and more people join in the squealing, and then the whole room is standing and squealing. I cover my ears and turn to Ralph, who seems as lost as I am. He frowns, looking around as if fearing everyone has lost their mind. Then he jumps on his feet, a wide grin replacing his frown.

"Someone found the bug," he mouths to me.

I'm not very aware of my next actions, but they include rising from my chair and uncovering my ears. The explosive sounds of cheering—and now clapping—doesn't bother me anymore. My head is spinning in a delirious swirl. I spot James on the side of the elevator. He's got his back turned to the room, one palm covering an ear, the other pressing his phone to his free ear. I'll have to wait to congratulate him. I search for Parker. It takes me a few minutes to locate him. He's still in front of a computer. Not the one he's been sitting at with James, but at one in the center of the room. He looks focused and determined, but no longer prone to start swearing. Next to him is a black-haired guy with glasses. By the way everyone pats his back, he must be the one who found the bug. The darned error in the code. I want to hug him.

"Okay," James's voice resounds after a few minutes. Everyone falls silent. "Parker and I need to meet up with the investors right away. How about all of you go over at Wellstone's and we'll meet you there later to celebrate?"

There is a general buzz of agreement in the room.

"Well done, everyone," James says.

Ralph is among the first to reach the elevator, already holding an unlit cigarette between his fingers. The room empties almost completely in the next ten minutes. It's just James and Parker who are left now, talking in low voices.

"Why don't you wait in the car, Parker? I'll join you in a minute."

"Don't be long," he says to James before leaving.

James walks up to me, grinning.

“Congratulations,” I say. “And sorry.”

“For what?”

“This was my fault. Ralph told me the investors were mad you forced Natalie out.”

"It’s true. I think that's what made them so ruthless with the deadline for fixing the bug. They liked Natalie and weren't exactly thrilled that I forced her out. They were looking for an excuse to… sever ties with me and the company. They might try again in the future. But I am not sorry. You are worth every risk."

I stare at him, my throat suddenly dry.

"You should go. You don't want to be late for your meeting with the investors. See you at breakfast to celebrate with the others." I am supposed to be at Stanford, but what the hell. He nearly bankrupted himself for me. I can skip a bloody class.

“Do I get one kiss for good luck?”

I grin, then tip my head forward, meeting his lips. When we break apart he murmurs, “I wish I could get on a jet with you and fly somewhere far away. Just the two of us." He lifts his hand to my face. As if reading my thoughts he says, “Don’t blame yourself too much. This kind of things happens in Silicon Valley all the time. It’s a very volatile environment.”

Shaking my head, I say, "I could never live like this. I don't know how you can."

"I couldn't imagine living any other way. It's the only way to live."

"You do agree that it's dangerous, though?"

His phone rings, and he puts it to his ear without glancing at the screen to see who's calling. "Yes Parker, I'll be there in a second." He closes the phone and smiles at me, walking backward toward the elevator.

"Of course it is dangerous. But it's also thrilling." He presses the elevator button, and the doors open immediately. "It makes me feel like I live life at its fullest every single moment. And what's the point, if you don't live life at its fullest? There is beauty in risk, Serena. I can show you that."

"I can't wait," I say, just before the elevator doors close, leaving me alone in the empty room. God, there is still so much adrenaline in this room.

I don't hate adrenaline; I just fear it. But part of me also relishes it. I felt that when I jumped from the plane. That small act of stepping into nothingness made me feel something I could get addicted to. Being with James is the most alive I've ever felt. I think a little adrenaline is exactly what I need. Smiling, I head toward the other elevator.

CHAPTER EIGHTEEN

I arrive with the group at Wellstone's, and James and Parker join us a while later, both grinning. The meeting with the investors went very well. After breakfast, James announces he has a surprise.

"I organized an outdoor day for the entire team and everyone else who helped."

"Oh," Parker says in surprise. "But everyone is so tired."

"Sleep is overrated."

On my left and right, two programmers, Nadine and David, sit up straight. I have a hunch they, too, think that sleep is overrated.

James grins. "Trust me, what I planned will shake them up for sure." He stands up and clears his throat. "Everyone, listen up. Two buses will arrive in about ten minutes. If you're up for some well-deserved fun, make sure you get on one." His voice vibrates with excitement and the promise of an adventure.

"Hell yeah," someone chants and others cheer as well.

As we wait, I pull out my phone to check my emails, and I'm pleasantly surprised to find a job offer from the bank in New York. *Holy shit.*

"Serena, anything wrong?" James asks. I pull him a little further away from the group, and hold my phone for him to see. His eyes widen.

"Congratulations, sweetheart."

"That's a lot of money. That salary is thirty percent higher than what the bank in San Francisco is offering."

"I knew you'd get the job." His voice is a little tight.

"I won't accept it, though."

I thought James would be relived, but instead he frowns. "Because of me?"

"Well, I told you I was never so keen and moving, but yes, Mr. Cohen, you can consider yourself a very important factor in my decision."

I'm expecting him to smile, but he does not. Hmm…what is happening?

"And you won't regret it further down the road?"

"I won't. I promise."

He's still *unhappy*. What on earth is wrong? I don't have time to coax the answer out of him, though, because the buses arrive.

I fall asleep in the bus, only waking up when it comes to a halt. Except for James and me, everyone is on their feet, waiting in line to get out.

"Where are we?" I ask James. Out the window, a vast river lies before my eyes.

"Tuolumne River."

I've never been to Tuolumne River, but I know roughly where it is on the map. "I slept for two hours?"

He smirks. "Two and a half, actually."

James and I get off the bus last. The first breath of air outside is refreshing. It isn't quite as cool as the AC in the bus, but it smells of pines. I'd like nothing better than to swim in the river. But the water flows so rapidly and there are so many rocks that I'm pretty sure I won't put as much as a toe in the water. I look around, trying to imagine what we could possibly do here. Wild would be the most appropriate word to describe this place. A plethora of pines and oaks populate the other shore of the river. The shore we're on is mostly grass and bushes that are a dry, pale yellow. Clouds of dust linger above the unpaved road behind us.

"This place doesn't really feel... celebratory," someone from the crowd shouts.

James's laughter echoes a few feet away from me.

My phone rings. I fish it out of the pocket of my slim jeans, and jolt a bit at the number on the screen. It's from England, but it's not my parents' number. My heart pounding hard, I try to remember who else has my number. Our neighbor, Ms. Tate, whom I gave it to in case of emergencies. But it can't be her; I have her number saved. Her name would appear on the screen if she'd be the one calling.

Biting my lip, I press the green button and hold the phone to my ear.

"I GOT the job," Jess shrieks in my ear. "I still can't believe it. I got it."

"Wow, that's amazing, Jess." I walk a little farther away from the buses, and make sure to keep the phone a few inches away from my ear because Jess's screams might deafen me. "How long do you have to decide if you accept it?"

"You're kidding, right? Hell, I've decided already. My place is here, hon. London is so much cooler than I thought. The people, the accent. God, this is just the perfect city. I can't believe you left."

"It was because of the rain, I told you," I joke, though a sinking feeling starts building in my stomach.

"Damn the rain."

"So when are you starting?"

For a few seconds, her heavy breaths are the only things I hear. "That's the only bad part. I start right after graduation."

I chuckle. Jess had planned one wild two-week-party marathon after graduation.

"I can't believe we'll live on different continents," Jess says. "I miss you already."

"I miss you too, Jess." It couldn't be truer and saying the words out loud only makes the feeling in my stomach worse.

"Serena," Parker yells from somewhere behind me, "come here."

"Was that Parker's voice?" Jess sneers.

"Yeah, I'm with him, James, and a bunch of other people. It's a long story. I'll tell you everything when you're back."

"You and James are so inseparable, I might get jealous."

I shove the phone back in my pocket and walk back to the group just as they start moving closer to the river.

Parker waits for me, hands in his pockets, a few feet away from everyone. "Come on," he urges.

"This is one lousy place for a party," I say.

He grins, as we follow the others down to the river. "Good thing then there won't be a party."

When we get close to the shore I look for

James. I find him standing right in front of the river, far away from us, talking to a teenage boy dressed in black overalls with a white shirt underneath. He's got exceptionally short, dark hair and looks vaguely familiar. I have a feeling the two of them are fighting. The boy's arms are folded over his chest. James has a deep frown on his forehead. It takes me a second to realize why the boy is looking so familiar. He's not a boy at all. She's wearing round silver earrings.

Dani.

She sees me too and waves at me, gesturing for me to come closer to them.

"What has she done—?"

"Don't say anything about the hair," Parker warns me.

"Right."

When I'm close enough, Dani says, grinning, "I didn't know you'd be here."

"I didn't know you'd be here either."

"That's because she's not supposed to be," James says through gritted teeth. "She's supposed to be at school."

Dani waves her hands, dismissing his words. "You really think I'd miss celebrating with you, and a good rafting trip?"

I gulp. Suddenly, the sound of water flowing isn't calming anymore, but menacing. "A what trip?" Neither of them pays attention to me.

"Since when are you into rafting?" James asks. "You've never wanted to come on rafting trips."

Dani stomps her foot. "Since now."

"How did you know we were coming here in the first place?" He frowns.

"You had your car brought here. And I... sneaked inside the car."

"Fantastic," James says, and I can't withhold a smile. "Well, forget about rafting. You're staying right here."

"I'd like to see you make me." Dani sticks her tongue out as James turns his back on her, heading back to the group. He squeezes my hand gently when he passes me, and the heat outside has nothing on the tingles of warmth that the soft touch of his skin sends through my entire body.

Dani looks at my hand with a knowing smile.

"So what about this rafting thing?" I ask her, biting the inside of my cheek.

"I'll tell you in a sec. I need your opinion on something. What do you think of my haircut?"

"Oh," I say, remembering Parker's warning. "Umm..."

Her smile drops a bit. "You don't like it?"

"It's just so... radical," I say.

"That's what I was aiming for," she exclaims proudly. "James says I look like a boy."

I couldn't agree more, but telling Dani so will surely break her heart. "You don't need anyone's approval to cut your hair the way you want it."

My answer brings a big grin to her face.

"I think it will perfectly match my new status as a college freshman," she says, clapping her hands excitedly. I smile at her. Her enthusiasm reminds me of Jess's before we started at Stanford. She didn't only get a new haircut, but also a tattoo. I didn't understand what all the fuss was about. I don't really understand it now either. Going to college wasn't really that much of a change. But maybe I've had the wrong idea about change all along. I went to great lengths to change everything around me after Kate died. I even changed my continent. But maybe things only really change when we decide to change. Maybe the secret to freeing ourselves from our past and our fears lies inside us. I spot James in the distance, and smile again.

"I am nervous about moving to England," Dani says. "I won't know anyone in England. Thank God Parker is moving back to London."

"When is he moving?"

"Today, actually. His plane leaves in a few hours."

I wink. "Jess will also be moving there."

"Jess, the friend with the bar accident?" Her

eyes light up. "That's wonderful. Jess seems to like going out a lot."

"That she does." I can't imagine someone better to help Dani become the party girl she wants to be.

"Did I hear someone mention Jess?" Parker asks, appearing by my side.

"She just called to tell me she got that job in London," I answer. "She'll be moving there soon."

Parker's face melts into a grimace, and I fight hard to withhold a laugh. Whatever caused the intense dislike between the two of them, it seems to be much more serious than I gave it credit.

"Come on, Parker." I elbow him. "There are quite a few people in London. I'm sure you'll manage to avoid each other."

"Why would you want to avoid Jess?" Dani asks, her eyebrows raised.

Parker scoffs.

If I'm honest, I'm pretty sure Jess won't want to avoid him forever. She'll seek him out just to annoy the hell out of him. That's always been her strategy when someone bothers her as badly as Parker: first avoid them, and then badger them with a vengeance. As I watch Parker and Dani, an image of the two of them and Jess having fun in London starts forming in my mind. Well, Jess and Dani having fun, and Jess annoying Parker to death.

"Has James changed his mind about letting me go rafting?" Dani asks Parker.

"I haven't talked to him about it."

Dani purses her lips, walking away.

"Will you please fill me in about the rafting thing?" I ask Parker, fidgeting my fingers behind my back.

"There's not much to fill you in on," he shrugs. "We'll grab rafts, wetsuits, and paddles, then go rafting on the river."

"On which river? Not this one, I hope. This looks like a deathtrap."

"Are you kidding? This is one of the best rivers for rafting in the U.S. Though I have to admit it's for more advanced rafters. Level four, I think."

I scrape my hand through my hair, biting my lip. "How many levels are there?"

"Six."

It's not Parker who answers, but James.

I turn around slowly, folding my arms over my chest. He's already wearing a blue wetsuit and a lopsided grin that takes my breath away.

"I'll go get a wetsuit," Parker excuses himself.

"Six levels, huh?" I mumble. "Well, you can count me out."

"This is absolutely not dangerous, Serena."

"Parker just said this is for advanced rafters. I've

never been rafting in my life."

"Which is why the rafts will be filled mostly with experienced rafters. There will only be one or two beginners in every raft. Besides, not the entire river is like this. There are large areas where the water is calmer and there are almost no rocks."

Staring at the river, it's hard to believe there are parts of it that look less deadly. I squirm in my spot, sinking half an inch in the mud below my feet.

"So you trusted me enough to jump from a plane with me, but you don't trust me with this?"

"Skydiving seemed safer," I say.

"Well," he muses, "to be honest, this is a *little* more dangerous than that. But it'll be a lot of fun."

"You didn't seem so willing to let Dani do it."

His eyes darken, and he shakes his head. "That's because Dani seems to be venturing into a lot of dangerous stuff lately. I don't want to encourage her."

"Sounds legit."

"So what, then?"

I stare behind him, shifting my weight from one foot to the other. The entire group is climbing into the half-dozen or so bright orange rafts that appeared on shore out of nowhere. Everyone is now dressed in the same blue wetsuit as James, and also wearing lifejackets and helmets, both as bright orange as the rafts.

"You fell for me," he says. "I assure you rafting is far less dangerous." James leans in to kiss me, and I intend to make a joke about him resorting to unfair tactics to get me to agree, but then I lose myself in the bliss is lips bring. When we gasp for air he murmurs, "Trust me to teach you to take risks safely, just like I trusted you to teach me how to forgive myself and love again."

"You love me?" I whisper.

"I do. With all my heart."

I smile as I say, "I love you too. And I'll do it."

As I follow him to the water, it occurs to me that the secret to freedom is trusting someone with my entire heart, while taking care of his too.

CHAPTER NINETEEN

When I climb into one of the rafts fifteen minutes later, I am positive I have never been so frightened in my life, despite being equipped with a lifejacket and helmet. There are four people on each side of the raft. I sit behind Parker and in front of James. Dani sits opposite me, pointedly ignoring James. I'm wearing a bathing suit (James ordered new ones to be bought for everyone especially for today) underneath my wetsuit, and all my clothes are now in the waterproof bag that I clutch for dear life. Parker takes the bag away from me, securing it at the back of the raft, and gives me a paddle instead.

I grip the paddle firmly and do my best to mimic Parker's smooth strokes, as the raft starts moving. Before I know it, we're speeding among the humongous gray rocks, and I pray we don't bump into one of them because the raft looks like it might not make it. My stomach tightens painfully when I look in front of us, because the river seems to be entirely made out of darned rocks. I grit my teeth when the inevitable collision nears, and close my eyes, expecting to be thrown out of the raft and possibly experience a healthy dose of pain.

Instead, nothing more than a shake-up and a splash of water follows. Everyone in the raft is cheering. I pretend to be cheering along with them and tighten my grip on the paddle.

"Your hands are going to get numb if you keep them like that," James whispers in my ear, sending an electrifying impulse through me. He puts his arm around my waist, pulling me closer to him. "Relax a bit and enjoy the scenery. It's beautiful out here."

I could do that, I just have to first convince myself that the giant rocks are made out of marshmallows. But as I feel James breathing on the back of my neck, my stomach loosens up a bit. Just a bit.

And then someone—Ralph, by the sound of his voice—shouts from the front of the raft.

"Okay, everybody, prepare yourselves. The first fall is coming."

"The first what?" I shout.

But as James abruptly withdraws his arm, I very well feel the what. I give up any pretense of paddling and just hold on tight to whatever I can, my eyes closed. My stomach tightens. Then the tightness transforms to lightness, surging to my chest in the free fall. Suddenly, all my senses are alert. The sound of water falling drums in my ears, the air—fresh and striking—fills my lungs, my chest.

The bump announcing the fall is over slams me into James. I open my eyes and find myself cheering along with everyone else. For real this time.

"What's the verdict? Fun or terrifying?" James asks.

I turn to him, grinning. "Terrifyingly fun?"

He leans in to me, a little too close. "You'd be up for it again?"

I hesitate just for a fraction of a second. "Absolutely."

"Good. Because a bigger fall will come farther down the river."

"Oh." I get up a bit, inspecting the water ahead of us, but the next fall must be much farther away, because I can't see anything. The river has changed. There are very few rocks as far as I can see, and the water itself is much calmer. I use this opportunity to take in the surroundings. James was right; this place really is beautiful. On the shore to the left lies a sea of green: oak trees and pines. To the right, the steep canyon wall towers over us, reflecting in the clear water.

"This is the base where we'll camp afterward," James says, showing me a point on the shore farther down. "But we'll go past it. We'll be going lower down the river and then we'll climb back to the base on foot."

"How long exactly is this trip going to last?" Parker asks. "I have a flight to catch."

"You'll make it to London all right, Parker" James answers. Within minutes, rocks appear in sight again; they're not like the ones before. They're sharper. More massive. And the water flows furiously among them.

"Ready?" James shouts.

"For what?"

"The next fall. It'll be in about four minutes."

I twist the paddle in my hands, looking ahead of us. A knot starts forming in my stomach as the water propels us forward, and rocks threaten us from both sides of the raft. But the knot isn't one of terror. It's one of. Yet as the raft swings us to the very edge and the fall stretches before me, the knot morphs into the light feeling I experienced before, during the last fall. And also, I realize, when I stepped out of that plane. Adrenaline.

And right now, I don't fear it. Not in the slightest. I welcome it. I want it. How is it that it is always around James that I change? What is it about him that makes me forget my fears and inhibitions, and become reckless?

I do manage to keep my eyes open this time when we dive into the free fall. The seconds that follow seem to take place in slow motion. The raft going downward. The water sprinkling in every direction, the drops scattering in a million pieces as they pierce the air, only to meld their way back into the river. I stretch out my hand to catch a few drops before they reach the surface of the river again. The lightning-quick beats of my heart—the only things playing out in real time it seems—drum in my ears.

I stretch out more, rising just a few inches from my seat and hear James cry, "Don't get up," before the raft gives its most violent jerk yet. I slip, and desperately try to grasp something—anything, to secure myself. I dig my nails into the edges of the raft. Another jolt follows and I slip again.

And fall right into the water.

A sharp pain tears through my right thigh, and I open my mouth to scream, but instead swallow a mouthful of water. My eyes are blurry and I have lost any sense of direction. I can't see the orange raft. Everywhere I look, sharp rocks point at me, and, as the stream pulls me in its midst, my only thought is, *I must not hit my head.*

I know I have a helmet, but I'm pretty sure the mere shock of colliding with a rock will be enough to make me pass out. I hold my arms around my head to protect it, and then something pulls at my arm, and I think, that's it, I'm a goner. But then the bright orange raft appears in front of me and I realize someone is pulling me back inside it.

All my limbs turn to rubber when I thump inside the raft. James holds me tight against his chest, and I cling to him, shaking, tears and water drops streaming down my face.

CHAPTER TWENTY

I close my eyes and rest my head against him as the raft comes to a halt and James lifts me in his arms. He steps on the shore and then sets me down on a wooden bench, taking off my helmet and putting it on the wooden picnic table behind me, next to his helmet and two waterproof bags. I recognize one of them as mine. I hope to God the bags are really waterproof, because I am soaked. And so is James.

"Are you hurt?" he asks, sitting on one knee in front of me. I can't tell if his voice is trembling or the nauseating throbbing inside my skull makes it seem that way. I look for the others, but there's no one in sight. It's only when I look at the river, and notice the orange raft sailing away, that I realize it's just the two of us here on shore.

"Where are the others going?" I mumble.

"Carrying on with the trip. I told them to drop us off here at the base. They'll arrive later."

I look around me, wondering what exactly he calls the base, since, except for the wooden bench and table, there's nothing but pines everywhere. A pathway stretches between the trees, and I wonder if the base is at the end of it, and if there's anyone there.

"Serena, are you hurt?" he repeats.

"No, I don't think so." But as I say the words, a spasm runs through my right thigh and I gasp.

"Let me take a look at it."

"It's nothing, really."

"Don't be silly. Let's get you out of this wetsuit."

Grudgingly, I stand up and peel the suit off me, until I'm all but naked in front of him; my cheeks feel so warm I'm pretty sure they're the same bright red as the tiny bikini I'm wearing.

"I always hated these crappy suits." He takes off his suit as well, standing before me in a pair of green shorts. I look away, my breath quickening.

"I'm so sorry about this," James says, eyeing my thigh as I slump back on the bench. One long scratch runs all the way to my knee.

"I'm an idiot, I should've held on tighter to the raft."

"It's my fault for pressuring you to come with us."

"I made the decision to come, James. It was my choice."

"You wouldn't have made that choice if it wasn't for me." Now that I've calmed down a little, I can see that he's completely beside himself. His gaze is haunted, his body is shaking. "When you were in the water, God, I was so scared."

His voice is shaking for real, and I have no idea what to tell him to calm him down.

"I'm fine, James. It was just a scare."

My words have no effect whatsoever. "What if it will be serious next time, huh?" He runs a frustrated hand through his hair, breathing in deeply. "I don't want to you to get hurt. I don't want to lose you."

I'm starting to panic, because James looks more desperate by the second. What is going on in that brilliant mind of his? Is he thinking about that time he lost Lara? Are old fears resurfacing?

"You won't lose me. I'll just be more careful. Accidents happen."

"Sometimes they're fatal."

"Sometimes they're not."

He taps his foot impatiently, pressing his palms against his eyes. When he takes them away, he looks more unsure than ever.

"You'd be so much better off without me," he murmurs.

I panic for real. "No, I wouldn't."

"I'm not good for you, Serena."

Okay, breathe in, breathe out. How do I reason with him? He seems to be lost in his fears, and I don't know how to change that.

"You are. You've made me happier than anyone ever has. You're a good man, James. I mean, look at today. You risked so much for me—your entire company."

"And now I was at the risk of losing you," he murmurs.

I trace the outline of his lips with my thumb, every cell in my body starting to burn for him. He's shaking. I'm shaking too. Like a leaf in the autumn breeze, like the drop of water trailing down his nose, to his lips, and then trickling on his chin, not in a straight, but twisted line, as if it's not quite sure of its course.

I am unsure of many things, but James' eyes darken, I become certain of one thing: this man will make love to me right here, right now.

I open my mouth to his in a breath-taking clash. He runs his tongue roughly over mine, his fingers digging in my hair. His other hand presses at the small of my back, holding me closer to him with a need as desperate as my own.

"James, are you sure no one is here?"

"Yes. I love you, Serena."

"I love you too," I murmur, pressing my lips to his in another kiss. I don't try to hide or control the quiver. I don't want to. I want to give into it, to lose myself in his words. So I do. His lips paint his words over my mouth, his hands carry them to my hips, his chest brings them closer to me with every breath.

I pull back a notch, just enough to see him, all of him. His beautiful eyes and full, wet lips, the shape of his statuesque torso and his strong arms. I want every inch of him carved in my memory. I want to take him in with all my senses. I start with the hollow of his neck, running my lips from there down onto his chest, my fingers drifting alongside, my nails leaving fine traces on his soft skin. His chest rumbles the lower I go. When I'm just below his navel, I stop and look up, pressing my lips to him just as my hand slides inside his boxers, caressing his erection. He groans in my mouth.

And then all our instincts break loose.

He hooks one arm around my waist, and pushes me on my back in the dirt, kissing me like never before. I don't know how, but I get rid of his shorts and then he's completely naked over me, and I'm completely naked in his arms. His tongue twists on my nipple, and his fingers torture me, first cupping my inner thigh, then circling their way up to my sex. I let out moan after moan as my body starts to pulsate and quiver, lightly in the beginning, then stronger and stronger until my whole body shakes.

"Please," I murmur against his lips when the emptiness inside me becomes too unbearable.

He thrusts into me and we both groan when our bodies unite in sheer abandon. I dig my nails deeply into his back when throbs of tension start rippling through me.

"Serena," he grunts in my ear, low and raspy, kissing my neck and the lobe of my ear. I push myself into him, desperately looking for pleasure, and the cadence of our moves becomes so frantic that I think our bodies might break. A knot forms in my stomach, because this feels like he's saying goodbye to me. I hope I'm wrong. God, I hope I'm wrong.

We clasp our hips against each other, giving into the unrelenting longing for relief. When his body goes rigid, and my own succumbs to an explosive orgasm, I press my mouth to his and claim his bliss.

He falls over me, and we stay like this, entangled, his head buried in my neck. Then he takes me into the river, and we refresh, putting our bathing suits back on. I'm a little afraid to look at him, because he hasn't said one word.

"James?" I ask tentatively when we get out of the water. "Is everything okay?"

He avoids my gaze, running his hand through

his hair. "I don't know."

"Talk to me," I plead.

He rubs his hands down his face, pressing his lips together. "I can't risk losing anyone else," he whispers.

"So instead you want to cut me out of your life?"

"You think this is easy for me? I love you Serena, and I didn't think I was capable of love anymore. But I can't shake off the feeling that you'd be better off without me. Safer, at least. You could explore all your opportunities. I wouldn't hold you back. You could go to New York if you wanted to."

"Don't make this about New York," I say angrily.

"It's not. It's about me not being able to be who you need."

"You're not making any sense." Panic crawls up my throat, and I suddenly feel cold.

"You're better off without me."

"Are you…are you breaking up with me?" I can't do this. I had a man push me out of his life before, and while I know that James isn't Michael, he's breaking my heart nonetheless.

"I just want what's best for you."

"Be a man and just say it," I hiss.

He looks at me sadly. "After you calm down,

you'll see that it's for the best."

"You're fucking unbelievable." I want to beat some sense into him, but I'm hurting too much to think straight. And if he really wants me out of his life, I can't humiliate myself and beg. Maybe this whole speech is just a way for him to let me down gently.

"I'll leave you to change. The camp is just between those trees." He turns around, walking in the direction he pointed, disappearing between the trees.

With trembling hands, I wipe the water off my skin, then take my clothes out of the waterproof bag, putting them on. *I will not cry. I will not cry.*

I need to get out of here, but how? I came on the bus with everyone. I remember that Parker said he needed to get to the airport. I'll catch a ride with him.

I don't go after James, instead sit down on the shore, waiting for the others to return. I cry silently, wiping at my tears. My heart grows so heavy that breathing becomes painful.

I have no idea how much time passes before everyone arrives, but as soon as Parker bids the group goodbye, I corner him.

"Can I catch a ride with you?" I ask. "I'll come to the airport and then take a cab to my apartment."

Parker looks at my eyes intently, and I think he can tell I've cried. "What's going on? Are you okay?"

"Your cousin is an idiot. I don't want to talk about it."

"Okay, come with me. James had his car brought here for this."

I manage to avoid James completely, and when I'm safely in the car, I take my first deep breath. I am silent most of the trip to the airport, lost in my thoughts. When we arrive, Parker explains, "Peter is here to take the car to James' penthouse. He can drop you off where you need."

I nod, feeling numb and sad. I want to go home, crawl in my bed and process what just happened.

Parker and I say hurried goodbyes, and just before he leaves, I remember about Jess.

"Hey, Jess is in London until tomorrow. Maybe you can meet up," I suggest. Parker throws me an uneasy glance. "Or not. The two of you will have a lot of fun once she moves there."

I ask Peter to drive me straight to the apartment. When I'm finally alone, one tear

rolls down my cheek. I don't bother to brush it away. More will come anyway. I slide down the door to my bedroom, giving in to sobs. The pain in my chest is raw and deep, and I can hardly breathe past it. I cry myself to sleep.

CHAPTER TWENTY-ONE

Over the next weeks, only one thing keeps me from completely shattering.

My old strategy: exhausting myself.

I exhaust myself to the point where I am so drained, I can't even think about him—or rather, his absence. During the day. The nights are an entirely different matter. Dreams invade my mind when it's most defenseless, leaving me drenched in sweat. Tears swell up in my eyes seconds after I wake up as I realize that none of the things in my dreams will ever be more than dreams again. I won't feel the touch of his lips on mine again, or hear him say my name in my ear in a low, urgent whisper.

James doesn't call, or attempt to make any kind of contact. When I lie awake at night, sometimes I have the urge to call him. Maybe I could make him understand. Or maybe he'd just push me away again, hurt me more.

As we approach graduation, Jess is ecstatic,

preparing for her move to London.

"I wish you'd come with me," she says.

"We'll keep in touch, Jess. That's what skype is for."

"Have you given New York more thought?"

"Nah. I turned it down and accepted the job in San Francisco. I like California, and I ran the numbers. Despite the higher salary, living in New York is more expensive, so I wouldn't have much more left over after everything is said and done."

"You're a smart cookie. And a tough cookie. I'm sorry about James."

I smile sadly. "Me too. But if he doesn't want to fight his fears, I can't fight them for him."

Jess hugs me tightly, sighing. "Men."

"Yeah. Men."

"But what would we do without them, eh?"

I laugh, pulling out of her arms. "I think I'm good on my own for a while."

"So…question. If James would get over himself, would you forgive him?"

I sit cross-legged on our couch, picking invisible lint off of it. "I love him, Jess. He hurt me, but I think we belong together. So, yes, if he wanted to give this a shot, I would be all for it. But I don't want to get my hopes up. I haven't even heard from him."

She nods in understanding, and changes the

subject to London again. Two days later, she announces, “We’re going out tonight.”

“But the graduation party is next week.”

“And tonight is Friday. I call it advance celebration,” she says with a wink. “I don’t know how much I’ll be able to party in London, so I’m going to party now.”

“Where are we going? Who else will be there?”

“Couple people from your lot, a couple from mine,” she says evasively. “We’re going to a fancy restaurant. Then we’ll go clubbing.”

“Since when do you like fancy restaurants?” I ask with skepticism.

“Hey, it’s a special occasion. Let’s get ready.”

One hour later, we sit in the back of a cab. He snorted when Jess told him the address, then asked us if we know that it's a very expensive place. Now he glares at our purses every few seconds, as if he's afraid we won't pay him. It would serve him right.

When we arrive I turn to Jess and smile, now excited for real. I can't imagine a better place to celebrate. The driver stops in front of the main entrance.

Just as I open the door, Jess tells the driver, "There's another entrance in the back where I need to be. Some of my friends are there."

"No there isn't—"

"I'm telling you there is," Jess snarls at him. "Serena dear, you should get out here. Aidan just texted me that he's in the back with some of the others. I'll go get them and meet you inside."

"No, no, I'll come with you."

"There's no need." She grins.

"Fine. See you in a bit." I pay the driver and step out of the car.

I climb the stairs to the entrance and smile widely as I take in the décor. It's minimalistic and classy, with a lot of glass and metal.

"Miss, you're not allowed to go in there," a woman says, appearing at the entrance.

"The restaurant is privately booked for tonight. I'm afraid you'll have to come back another day. I'll be happy to make a reservation for you."

"Thanks," I say, doing a very bad job of hiding my disappointment. I'm about to call Jess to tell her that we should spread the word that nothing is happening anymore when I see *him*, sitting in one of the two armchairs across the room, in front of the fireless fireplace. The amused expression on his face tells me he's been watching me for a while.

CHAPTER TWENTY-TWO

"What are you doing here?" I ask blankly.

He gets up from the armchair and walks toward me with determined, but slow-paced, strides, holding his hands behind his back. "I heard there was something to celebrate."

"Not anymore. Haven't you heard the second part? The place is privately booked."

"I know." He smiles, pulling gently at the sleeves of his black shirt. "I booked it."

I fold my arms over my chest. "I see. I take it that Jess didn't actually invite anyone else and that if I call her now, she's already on her way to our apartment?"

"No, she's on her way to downtown San Jose actually, meeting the crowd there. I believe the words *partying all night* have come up twice in our conversation."

"I see. So what now?"

"Now we talk."

"You booked the entire place so you could talk to me?" I ask incredulously.

"I thought you'd be more comfortable without other people around."

James leads us to a table in the center of the room, and I nervously sit down.

"What is this about?" I ask once he's opposite me.

He taps his fingers on the table, but doesn't answer as a waiter arrives to pour us drinks. Once we're alone, he says, "I want to apologize. For hurting you, for giving in to my fears."

"You pushed me away," I whisper.

"I made a mistake. I cannot take that back, and I cannot change it. But you know what? That is one mistake I don't regret."

I gasp, a burning sensation starting to form behind my eyelids.

James shakes his head, grabbing both my hands in his over the table. "That didn't come out right. What I meant was that I do regret, from the bottom of my heart, that I hurt you. But pushing you away made me realize that I can't be without you. I love you, Serena."

I blink, then blink again. God, I want to believe his words so much. But I'm also afraid.

"Why now? Why haven't you called?"

"Honestly, I needed time to work things out in

my head. I wasn't in a good place. Then I was convinced you wouldn't even want to talk to me. But a mutual friend told me differently."

"Jess."

"Yep," he confirms.

"I wonder how long she waited to call you after our conversation. What's to say you won't make other mistakes like this? I can't bear the thought that something… unpleasant… might happen between us, and you'll just run again."

"It won't happen again. You have my word. I know I wasn't rational. I let old fears get the better of me."

"I love you," I whisper. "I want us to work out."

"We will. You make me feel things that I haven't felt with anyone else. Things I didn't even know I could feel. Your kisses… you have no idea what your kisses have done to me, Serena. How they've healed me… I—I never feel as whole as when I make love to you. A smile from you can make everything better. It's the first time I spend more time thinking of someone else than I do of myself. And it feels damn good. There's nothing I'd rather do in this life than make you happy. Your happiness is everything to me."

His words are like a balm to me. They fill my mind, my body… every cell of it.

“Please say that you forgive me, that you want to give me—us—another shot.”

“I do. God, I want nothing more than to love you.”

He tightens his grip on my hands, his eyes never leaving mine. "I don't want us to be apart ever again. These weeks were the worst of my life. I couldn't sleep, or do any fucking thing right. I worked twenty hours a day just to exhaust myself so I won't think about you all the time." I catch my breath. I had almost forgotten how alike we are, he and I. Addicted to movies and exhaustion. Addicted to each other. He moves his chair on my side of the table, cupping my face in his hands and pulling me into a kiss. It’s slow and sweet, and I can’t get enough.

“You are perfect for me, Serena McLewis. He takes both my hands in his, looking down at them. "I'm sorry I clung so tightly to the past. That I allowed it to terrify me so much. Losing someone we love shapes us, punches us in the gut until we bend and break. But we must never let that pain define us." He blinks up at me. Smiling. "Thank you for showing me that," he whispers, and I catch my breath as he tucks a strand of hair behind my ear.

We eat quickly, and I can’t even say I’m paying attention to the food. I’m beyond happy that this wonderful man and I found our way back to each other. And I can't wait to be alone with him. We even skip dessert.

Once we're at his car, he opens the door for me, but before I can climb in, he says,

"What would you say about a spontaneous trip? The airport isn't far away."

He pulls me to him, wrapping his arms around me, holding me tightly to him, the warmth of his body fusing with mine, breathing life into me.

For a few seconds, neither of us moves. We just stand, entangled in each other's arms, eyes locked. Then his soft lips cover mine. Relief pours from his lips, reverberates from his chest, as his hands cup my face, bringing a warmth to my cheeks that spreads slowly throughout my body, filling all of me, from my core to the tips of my fingers.

We break off gasping for air, but neither pulls too far away. I need to have him close. I need to feel his warm breath on my lips. He presses his forehead to mine, and I relish the moment, my eyes closed. We both burst out laughing.

"So, how about that trip? Just for the weekend?"

"I don't have a passport. Or clothes."

"A mutual friend took care of that. There is a backpack in the trunk for you."

I poke his chest. "You were awfully convinced

this would work out.”

“I hoped it would, and I wanted to be prepared to sweep you off your feet.”

“That’s so sweet.” I shift my gaze back to his lips. "A trip sounds tempting."

His grin widens, and just when I think he will lean in and kiss me, he steps away from me. "Let's go then."

"Where are we going?"

The corner of his lips lift into a half-smile. "Where would be the fun if I told you?"

EPILOGUE: JAMES

"Stop frowning," Serena says. "You'll get wrinkles."

We're at L'Etoile, which has become our go-to restaurant after a long day at work. Serena started working this summer, and her schedule is just as crazy as mine.

"I'm not sure I should have allowed Dani to move in with Jess," I say. Dani moved to England two months ago. She was supposed to go to Oxford, which is located in a small town I very much approved of. But her rebellion led to her missing the grades Oxford required, so she now goes at a London university. To top it all, she and Jessica decided that since they'll both move there on their own, they might as well live together.

Serena pinches her nose in that adorable way she does when she doesn't agree with me. It's good that she doesn't always agree. I like a dare, and no challenge is sweeter than when it comes from my woman.

"Stop being so over-protective. Dani's eighteen, James. She doesn't need your permission. Who knows, maybe it won't be a disaster."

I raise an eyebrow as I look at my phone, scanning the photo Dani just posted on social media. She and Jess are out and about in London. To my astonishment, Jess is dressed more decently than my sister. When I turn the screen of my phone to Serena, she laughs softly.

"Dani is a good girl trying to turn bad. Jess is a bad girl trying to turn good. They'll manage."

"I hope so." Putting my phone away, I turn my attention to her.

"There is always Parker to keep an eye on them."

It's my turn to laugh. "Ahh, I am not sure Parker can handle Jessica."

"Can I tell you a secret?" Serena drops her voice to a whisper. "I think Parker actually *likes* Jessica."

"Well, I'll be very impressed if that's true. I haven't seen Parker date anyone in a long time."

"I think Jess is up for a challenge."

"Here is your dessert," the waitress announces, putting down the chocolate fondue in front of Serena. As always, her eyes lighten up as she digs in. No matter how many times she orders this, she has the same look of longing when it arrives.

"Aren't you going to eat any dessert? You must still be hungry, you barely ate," she says.

I lean toward her over the table, watching her straight in the eyes. "I'm hungry for you."

I watch with satisfaction the blush spreading on her cheeks. My need for her is insatiable. The more time I spend with her, the more I want her. I grow restless at the office when we're apart, but find peace again every night when I'm with her. She taught me how to forgive myself. Next to her, I became whole again. For all my risk-taking, I wasn't willing to take the biggest risk of all: falling in love again. Until I met her. She loves me with an intensity that demands everything, so that's what I give her. Every night I love her more, and every day I miss her more. Luckily, she's not going anywhere. I watch her eat in silence, contemplating all the ways I am going to make love to her tonight.

When we arrive home, one hour later, I can't contain my grin as I place my hands on her hips and turn her around to face me. I drag my fingers down her cheek, then along the contour of her lips. Feeling her hot, short breaths on my skin makes my pulse ratchet up. She wants me just as much as I want her.

"Why are you looking so excited?" she whispers as I lean in to kiss her.

"Because now I'm about to have dessert."

"The things you say. You make me immensely happy, James."

I kiss her chin, then her bottom lip. "And I plan to do it for the rest of our lives."

***

THE END

***

OTHER BOOKS BY LAYLA HAGEN

The Lost Series

Found in Us

Jessica Haydn wants to leave her past behind. Hurt by one too many heartbreaks, she vows not to fall in love again. Especially not with a man like Parker, whose electrifying pull and smile bruised her ego once before. But his sexy British accent makes her crave his touch, and his blue eyes strip Jessica of all her defenses.

Parker Blakesley has no place for love in his life. He learned the hard way not to trust. He built his business empire by avoiding distractions, and using sheer determination and control. But something about Jessica makes him question everything. Not only has she a body made for sin, but her laughter fills a void inside of him.

The desire igniting between them spirals into an unstoppable passion, and so much more. Soon, neither can fight their growing emotional connection. But can two scarred souls learn to trust again? And when a mistake threatens to tear

them apart, will their love be strong enough?
AVAILABLE ON ALL RETAILERS

Caught in Us

Dani Cohen knows Damon is trouble the second he walks in during senior year. He has bad boy written all over him … from his arrogant smirk to his perfectly toned abs. He is arrogant, intense, rebellious.

Dani has her future all planned out. She's not the type to fall for a bad boy, no matter how his panty-melting grin is or how shamelessly he flirts. But something about Damon draws her in, awakening a desire she's never felt. Slowly, she uncovers the secrets Damon hides: underneath his arrogance lies a tortured soul, his flirting smile masks despair.

Damon arrives in Dani's life against his will. Carrying the scars of a dark past and facing an uncertain future, he knows he should stay away from her, but can't. Her innocence consumes him, as does the desire to indulge in the passion igniting deep inside her.

An all-consuming bond blooms into a reckless love. But when mistakes from the past threaten their already fragile future, can their love survive?

AVAILABLE ON ALL RETAILERS

OTHER BOOKS BY LAYLA HAGEN

The Bennett Family Series

Book 1: Your Irresistible Love (Sebastian & Ava)

Book 2: Your Captivating Love (Logan & Nadine)

Book 3: Your Forever Love (Pippa & Eric)

Book 4: Your Inescapable Love (Max & Emilia)

Book 5: Your Tempting Love (Christopher & Victoria)

Book 6: Your Alluring Love (Alice & Nate)

Book 7: Your Fierce Love (Blake & Clara)

Book 8: Your One True Love (Daniel & Caroline)

Book 9: Your Endless Love (Summer & Alex)

Book 1 in the Series: Your Irresistible Love

Sebastian Bennett is a determined man. It's the secret behind the business empire he built from scratch. Under his rule, Bennett Enterprises dominates the jewelry industry. Despite being ruthless in his work, family comes first for him, and he'd do anything for his parents and eight siblings—even if they drive him crazy sometimes. . . like when they keep nagging him to get married already.

Sebastian doesn't believe in love, until he brings in external marketing consultant Ava to oversee the next collection launch. She's beautiful, funny, and just as stubborn as he is. Not only is he obsessed with her delicious curves, but he also finds himself willing to do anything to make her smile.

He's determined to have Ava, even if she's completely off limits.

Ava Lindt has one job to do at Bennett Enterprises: make the next collection launch unforgettable. Daydreaming about the hot CEO is definitely not on her to-do list. Neither is doing said CEO. The consultancy she works for has a strict policy—no fraternizing with clients. She won't risk her job. Besides, Ava knows better than to trust men with her heart.

But their sizzling chemistry spirals into a deep

connection that takes both of them by surprise. Sebastian blows through her defenses one sweet kiss and sinful touch at a time. When Ava's time as a consultant in his company comes to an end, will Sebastian fight for the woman he loves or will he end up losing her?

AVAILABLE ON ALL RETAILERS.

Book 2 in the Series: Your Captivating Love

Logan Bennett knows his priorities. He is loyal to his family and his company. He has no time for love, and no desire for it. Not after a disastrous engagement left him brokenhearted. When Nadine enters his life, she turns everything upside down.

She's sexy, funny, and utterly captivating. She's also more stubborn than anyonc he's met…including himself.

Nadine Hawthorne is finally pursuing her dream: opening her own clothing shop. After working so hard to get here, she needs to concentrate on her new business, and can't afford distractions. Not even if they come in the form of Logan Bennett.

He's handsome, charming, and doesn't take no for an answer. After bitter disappointments, Nadine doesn't believe in love. But being around Logan is addicting. It doesn't help that Logan's family is scheming to bring them together at every turn.

Their attraction is sizzling, their connection undeniable. Slowly, Logan wins her over. What starts out as a fling, soon spirals into much more than they are prepared for.

When a mistake threatens to tear them apart,

will they have the strength to hold on to each other?

AVAILABLE ON ALL RETAILERS.

Book 3 in the Series: Your Forever Love

Eric Callahan is a powerful man, and his sharp business sense has earned him the nickname 'the shark.' Yet under the strict façade is a man who loves his daughter and would do anything for her. When he and his daughter move to San Francisco for three months, he has one thing in mind: expanding his business on the West Coast. As a widower, Eric is not looking for love. He focuses on his company, and his daughter.

Until he meets Pippa Bennett. She captivates him from the moment he sets eyes on her, and what starts as unintentional flirting soon spirals into something neither of them can control.

Pippa Bennett knows she should stay away from Eric Callahan. After going through a rough divorce, she doesn't trust men anymore. But something about Eric just draws her in. He has a body made for sin and a sense of humor that matches hers. Not to mention that seeing how adorable he is with his daughter melts Pippa's walls one by one.

The chemistry between them is undeniable, but the connection that grows deeper every day that has both of them wondering if love might be within their reach.

When it's time for Eric and his daughter to head

back home, will he give up on the woman who has captured his heart, or will he do everything in his power to remain by her side?

AVAILABLE ON ALL RETAILERS.

Book 4 in the series: Your Inescapable Love

A steamy and swoony friends-to-lovers romance

Max Bennett is a successful man. His analytical mind has taken his family's company to the next level. Outside the office, Max transforms from the serious business man into someone who is carefree and fun. Max is happy with his life and doesn't intend to change it, even though his mother keeps asking for more grandchildren. Max loves being an uncle, and plans to spoil his nieces rotten.

But when a chance encounter reunites him with Emilia, his childhood best friend, he starts questioning everything. The girl he last saw years ago has grown into a sensual woman with a smile he can't get out of his mind.

Emilia Campbell has a lot on her plate, taking care of her sick grandmother. Still, she faces everything with a positive attitude. When the childhood friend she hero-worshipped steps into her physical therapy clinic, she is over the moon. Max is every bit the troublemaker she remembers, only now he has a body to drool over and a smile to melt her panties. Not that she intends to do the former, or let the latter happen.

They are both determined not to cross the boundaries of friendship…at first. But as they spend more time together, they form an undeniable bond and their flirty banter spirals out of control.

Max knows Emilia is off-limits, but that only makes her all the more tempting. Besides, Max was never one to back away from a challenge.

When their chemistry becomes too much to resist and they inevitably give in to temptation, will they risk losing their friendship or will Max and Emilia find true love?

AVAILABLE ON ALL RETAILERS.

Book 5 in the series: Your Tempting Love

Christopher Bennett is a persuasive man. With his magnetic charm and undeniable wit, he plays a key role in the international success of his family's company.

Christopher adores his family, even if they can be too meddling sometimes… like when they attempt to set him up with Victoria, by recommending him to employ her decorating services. Christopher isn't looking to settle down, but meeting Victoria turns his world upside down. Her laughter is contagious, and her beautiful lips and curves are too tempting.

Victoria Hensley is determined not to fall under Christopher's spell, even though the man is hotter than sin, and his flirty banter makes her toes curl. But as her client, Christopher is off limits. After her parents' death, Victoria is focusing on raising her much younger siblings, and she can't afford any mistakes. . .

But Victoria and Christopher's chemistry is not just the sparks-flying kind. . .It's the downright explosive kind. Before she knows it, Christopher is training her brother Lucas for soccer tryouts and reading bedtime stories to her sister Chloe.

Victoria wants to resist him, but Christopher is determined, stubborn, and oh-so-persuasive.

When their attraction and connection both spiral out of control, will they be able to risk it all for a love that is far too tempting?

AVAILABLE ON ALL RETAILERS.

Book 6 in the series: Your Alluring Love

Alice Bennett has been holding a torch for her older brother's best friend, Nate, for more than a decade. He's a hotshot TV producer who travels the world, never staying in San Francisco for too long. But now he's in town and just as tempting as ever… with a bossy streak that makes her weak in the knees and a smile that melts her defenses.

As a successful restaurant owner, Alice is happy with her life. She loves her business and her family, yet after watching her siblings find their happy ever after, she can't help feeling lonely sometimes—but that's only for her to know.

Nate has always had a soft spot for Alice. Despite considering the Bennetts his family, he never could look at her as just his friend's little sister. She's a spitfire, and Nate just can't stay away. He loves making her laugh… and blush.

Their attraction is irresistible, and between stolen kisses and wicked-hot nights, they form a deep bond that has them both yearning for more.

But when the chance of a lifetime comes knocking at his door, will Nate chase success even if it means losing Alice, or will he choose her?

AVAILABLE ON ALL RETAILERS.

Book 7 in the series: Your Fierce Love

The strong and sexy Blake Bennett is downright irresistible. And Clara Abernathy is doing everything she can to resist his charm.

After spending her life in group homes, Clara yearns for the love and warmth of a true family. With the Bennetts treating her like their own, she can't possibly fall for Blake. That would be crossing a line…

But when Clara needs a temporary place to live, and she accepts Blake's offer to move next door to him, things escalate. Suddenly, she's not only supposed to resist the man who's hell-bent on having her, but the TV station she works for is determined to dig up some dirt on the Bennett family.

Blake knows family friends are off-limits, and Clara is more off-limits than anyone. But Clara's sweetness and sass fill a hole in him he wasn't even aware of. Soon, he finds himself gravitating toward her, willing to do anything to make her happy.

Blake enjoys bending the rules—much more than following them, but will bending this one be taking it too far?

AVAILABLE ON ALL RETAILERS.

Book 8 in the Series: Your One True Love

She's the one who got away. This time, he refuses to let her slip through his fingers.

Daniel Bennett has no regrets, except one: letting go of the woman he loved years ago. He wouldn't admit it out loud, but he's been pining for Caroline ever since. But his meddling family can read him like an open book. So when his sisters kick up their matchmaking shenanigans, Daniel decides to play right along. After all, he built his booming adventure business by making the most out of every opportunity. And he doesn't intend to miss an opportunity to be near Caroline.

Caroline Dunne knows better than to fall for Daniel again. But his seductive charm melts her determination to keep her heart in check. Even with their lives going in separate directions, neither can ignore the magnetic pull between them.

But will they find the second chance they've both wanted all along?

AVAILABLE ON ALL RETAILERS.

Book 9 in the Series: Your Endless Love

An incurable romantic with a chronic case of bad luck with men…

Museum curator Summer Bennett knows that happily-ever-afters are not make-believe. After all, her siblings all found their soulmates, so she's optimistic her prince charming will come along too…eventually. In the meantime, she focuses on her job and her volunteering—which brings her face to face with one of Hollywood's hottest A-listers.

When Alexander Westbrook flashes America's favorite panty-melting smile, Summer's entire body responds. When she asks him to get involved in the community where she volunteers, Summer is shocked that the Hollywood heartthrob agrees right away. Two weeks working side by side with the world's sexiest guy, and the game is on.

Far from the public eye, Summer discovers she likes the real Alex even more than his on-screen persona. Secret kisses and whispered conversations spark a fire in her that nothing can extinguish. If only his life wasn't splashed all over the tabloids…

Alex can't keep his eyes–or his hands–off of Summer. But she's too sweet, and too damn lovely to be swept up in his Hollywood drama. His career is at risk, and an iron-clad clause in his contract with the studio makes a relationship impossible. But staying away from her is out of the question.

AVAILABLE ON ALL RETAILERS

The Connor Family Series

Book 1: Anything For You

Anything For You
Book 1: The Connor Family Series
Sexy. Sweet. Unapologetically Romantic

Hotshot CEO Landon Connor knows what he wants: success. He knows his way around the boardroom, and his work has been front and center for him ever since losing his wife. But after sealing the biggest deal of his career, he decides to take a trip to his hometown. Nothing spells vacation like a little time in the LA sun with the boisterous family he's missed so much.

But the tempting landscape designer working for his sister spells a whole lot more than fun. Maddie Jennings is everything Landon didn't think he wanted anymore. He can't get enough of Maddie's sweetness, or her sensual curves, and he pursues her every chance he gets.

Despite fanning herself every time Landon comes near her, Maddie tries to ignore their attraction. But Maddie hasn't met anyone quite like Landon. He's sexier than anyone has the right to be, and more intense too.

When Landon romances her with late night

walks and flowers, she can't help giving in to him. His touch is intoxicating, and his love is beautiful.

But can Landon open up his heart for longer than a summer?

AVAILABLE ON ALL RETAILERS.

Standalone USA TODAY BESTSELLER Withering Hope

Aimee's wedding is supposed to turn out perfect. Her dress, her fiancé and the location—the idyllic holiday ranch in Brazil—are perfect.

But all Aimee's plans come crashing down when the private jet that's taking her from the U.S. to the ranch—where her fiancé awaits her—defects mid-flight and the pilot is forced to perform an emergency landing in the heart of the Amazon rainforest.

With no way to reach civilization, being rescued is Aimee and Tristan's—the pilot—only hope. A slim one that slowly withers away, desperation taking its place. Because death wanders in the jungle under many forms: starvation, diseases. Beasts.

As Aimee and Tristan fight to find ways to

survive, they grow closer. Together they discover that facing old, inner agonies carved by painful pasts takes just as much courage, if not even more, than facing the rainforest.

Despite her devotion to her fiancé, Aimee can't hide her feelings for Tristan—the man for whom she's slowly becoming everything. You can hide many things in the rainforest. But not lies. Or love.

Withering Hope is the story of a man who desperately needs forgiveness and the woman who brings him hope. It is a story in which hope births wings and blooms into a love that is as beautiful and intense as it is forbidden.

AVAILABLE ON ALL RETAILERS.

Published by Layla Hagen

Published: Layla Hagen 2018

***

Acknowledgements

Publishing a book takes a village! A big THANK YOU to everyone accompanying me on this journey. To my family, thank you for supporting me, believing in me, and being there for me every single day. I could not have done this without you.

Excerpt from Found in Us

CHAPTER ONE
Jessica

Dresses come in three lengths, as far as I'm concerned: stay-away-from-me length, buy-me-a-drink length, and take-me-home-with-you length. Mine is somewhere between the last two, though I don't intend to entice anyone to buy me a drink, much less take me home.

Old habit, I suppose.

I lean forward to the cabbie and say, "Mayfair, please."

He nods, smiling at me and Dani, my roommate, in the rearview mirror. Dani pulls a bit at her own dress, as if desperately trying to make the fabric appear a few good inches longer. Her skirt is definitely take-me-home-with-you length. She looks as uncomfortable in it as she was when she first tried it on, but she insisted on wearing it. That's what college girls wear, she said, with an enthusiasm that only a freshman can muster. The red fabric does look gorgeous on her, though, contrasting beautifully with her dark, very short bob.

I stare out the window, nostalgic about my own college days, which ended only one month ago. I moved from California to London right after graduating from Stanford. I have loved this city to pieces since the first time I was here. Two months later, my fascination hasn't lessened one bit. I'm starting to think it never will. I love everything about it: from the never-slowing pulse of the city to the downright moody weather. There is no reason to dislike London.

Well, maybe one, but I'd rather not think about it right now. However, Dani's next words force me to do just that.

"I hope Parker isn't there already. He doesn't like it when I'm late."

I turn to her slowly. "Parker is joining us at the bar tonight?" I ask.

"Yes." She blushes furiously. "Sorry, Jess . . . forgot to tell you."

I sigh, leaning back in my seat. I haven't seen Parker in a while, but I know I can't avoid him; he is Dani's cousin, after all. I met him a few months ago when he was in the US, working with Dani's brother, James. I think my reaction when I first saw him is best summed up by the word stunned. I can think of a few more words to describe him, though. Scorching hot. Infuriating idiot. The last part became obvious only after I was around him several times.

I straighten up when we enter the bar, pushing

my long, blonde hair to one side. Though the decor is minimalist, with a dozen or so low tables surrounded by couches, the place has a far more elegant feel than I expected. All the tables are occupied, except the one right next to the bar. Dani says she'll join me there in a second; she needs to go to the bathroom. I stop at the bar and order a cocktail—a mojito—then proceed to the table and slump on the couch, running my fingers on the dark leather beneath me. I swallow the first sip, close my eyes, and savor the moment. I've done this a lot since I moved here. But patting oneself on the back from time to time should be mandatory, especially when there's no one else around to do it. Achievements should be celebrated. Best with booming music and tequila shots. But a mojito in a quiet, fancy bar will do as well. I suppose this is how responsible people celebrate. Which is exactly what I'm trying to be. I have the job I want at a modern art and history museum, and I moved to this city I love. It's a good feeling, being independent at twenty-two. I'm still working on the being responsible part.

"I want a gin and tonic." I hear a man's voice behind me order the bartender and instantly open my eyes. *That British accent, my God.* I know who the voice belongs to. Low and commanding and somehow always strong enough to get everyone around him to do what he wants.

And apparently quicken my pulse.

When he finally comes into view, I suck in a deep breath. His dark blond hair is slightly longer than the last time I saw him, and it frames his handsome face perfectly. He's wearing a black suit—an Armani, I think—with a white dress shirt underneath it.

All man.

The kind of man that makes any decent woman fantasize for hours about doing less-than-decent things to him. Me included.

His blue eyes widen in surprise when he sees me, and as he lazily undoes the only button of his jacket, throwing it on the couch opposite me, says, "Finally ran out of excuses to avoid me, Jessica?"

"I wasn't avoiding you, Parker. I was busy. I've had lots of things to take care of since I moved here. Important things."

He shakes his head almost imperceptibly, saying, "So how are you finding London? Is it living up to your dream?" He eyes me from head to toe as he sits down, and every inch of my skin catches fire under his gaze.

"I should say so," I say, sipping from my mojito. "The apartment is beautiful. I love my job at the museum. Men around here aren't too bad, either."

This catches his attention. In a fraction of a

second, his eyes snap up from my hips and meet my own eyes. He puts his gin and tonic on the table.

"Been hunting already? Be careful who you pick, Jessica. I might not be around like last time to keep your spontaneity from hurting you."

Now *this* is the Parker I know.

Presumptuous.

Infuriating.

"I don't need you to save me, Parker." I do a damn lousy job at keeping my voice even. Though truth be told, I did need saving that one time he's referring to. And saving me cost him a split lip and a black eye. I didn't emerge unscathed that night, though that was the direct result of my idiocy and dismal eye-hand coordination rather than a fight. We were in a club, and some guy didn't like when I told him no. Parker stepped in, and things escalated.

Parker leans a few inches over the table and says in a low voice, "Who said I have any intention to *save* you?"

His gaze pierces me and I stubbornly hold it, feeling my cheeks getting hotter. He breaks his gaze at last, lowering it slowly, very slowly to my cleavage and then to my hips, as if he's drinking me in. I cross my legs and let out an involuntary sigh. Parker's breath catches. I look away, not daring to meet his eyes.

Luckily, Dani arrives, cutting some of the tension.

"Parker, you're here already," she exclaims. Parker gets up and places a gentle kiss on each of her cheeks. "See," she says to him, smiling proudly, "I told you I'd eventually get Jess to go out with us."

The slightest flush crosses Parker's features, but he recovers quickly and says, "I was concerned Jessica was overworking herself."

Dani grins. "You're a gentleman, as always." Bless her. She and, as far as I can tell, everyone else who knows him, seems to be utterly convinced that Parker is the ultimate gentleman. I'm convinced he's the ultimate man, all right. It's just the gentle part I'm not convinced of.

"I'll get myself a gin and tonic," Dani says after taking a sip from Parker's glass.

"I can get you one," he offers.

"No, no, it's fine," she says, hurrying to the bar.

He frowns as he glances at her, then asks in a tone so full of concern, it startles me, "How is she?"

"What do you mean?" I ask.

"James is concerned about her. So am I."

"Well, he's her older brother, so he has an excuse. But I think you are both overreacting.

She's a perfectly normal young girl who wants to have some fun." Actually, there is no way for me to know if that's true. I don't know Dani very well. I met her at the same time I met Parker, but unlike Parker, whom I met very often afterward, I didn't see Dani much. The decision to move in together in London was more of an I-don't-know-anyone-else-in-London case.

Dani comes back with her drink, and just as Parker opens his mouth, the background music suddenly grows louder, and someone—the DJ probably, though I can't see him anywhere—says through the speakers, "Let the fun part of the evening begin, ladies and gentlemen."

The slowest blues in the history of the world starts playing.

"This is fun?" I ask incredulously, as some couples leave the couches and start dancing in the center of the room to the painfully boring song.

"It can be," Parker says, standing up. "Dani, excuse us for a few minutes."

"By all means," Dani says, grinning.

Parker turns to me. "Come on, let's dance."

"I don't dance to this kind of music," I say dismissively. "It bores me to tears."

He fixes me with his gaze and I choke on my next breath. "You will dance with me."

A slight tremble shakes me as I follow him to

the dance floor.

"I promise you it will be anything but boring." Parker puts an arm around my waist, and with a jolt pulls me so close to him that our chests touch. No one is dancing *this* close. As we start dancing, he interlaces his left hand with mine, as if nothing would be more natural. I swallow hard, burning at the points where our bare skin touches. I rest my left hand on his chest, taking in his solid frame. I had guessed he was well built. It's not hard to guess really. The contour of his toned arms and chest is discernible even through the long-sleeved shirts he usually wears. Touching him like this, though . . . I bite my lip. Behind his shoulder, I see Dani beaming at us. This reminds me of her comment and how it put Parker on the spot.

"So you were worried I was overworking myself? Thinking about me, were you?" I ask playfully, hoping if I keep him talking, he won't feel the hammering of my heart against his chest.

"I was, Jessica," he whispers in my ear, sending burning tingles down my spine.

I draw a deep breath, but that only manages to liquefy me further. He's not wearing any cologne. The smell of *him* emanates from every pore; his scent is intoxicating.

He pulls back a notch, biting his lip. I have the sudden urge to run my fingers through his thick hair, pull him to me, and taste those darned lips. Bite them, kiss them. I only realize he's been watching me fantasize about his lips when he says in a low, husky voice, "I've been thinking about you, I admit it. And I—"

I shriek, jumping away from Parker, as someone collides with us and spills a drink with ice cubes right on my chest.

"I am so sorry," a woman in her mid-thirties, holding an almost empty glass says, eyeing my dress in horror. One glance at my white dress and I realize why. Her drink had some kind of red fruit blended in it, which pretty much means I can kiss this dress goodbye.

"Okay, I need to clean this mess," I say in what I hope is a measured tone. As I swirl on my heels in the direction of the door, I catch Parker trying to stifle a laugh.

The bathroom is one hell of a twisted corridor away from the bar. If it weren't for the fluorescent signs marking the way to it, I doubt I'd find it at all. I curse all the way, but as I waste tissue after tissue in front of one of the sleek sinks, I think maybe a cold shower is exactly what I need. Things with Parker were getting . . . I don't know what, but they were getting. . .something. I shake my head. No, I thought that once before, and then, despite sizzling chemistry floating in the air,

Parker made it painfully clear there was nothing between us. On a night very different from this one, Parker did one of the most insulting things you can do to a woman—or at least to me—he brushed me off. Plain and simple, he rejected me.

Why he did it, I never found out. Not that it matters. All that matters is that I continue to do exactly what I've been doing until now: stay away from him. I need to focus on my new life here. Somehow, guys have always messed up things for me. *Because I allowed them to mess things up,* I remind myself. Starting with my dad, down to every single asshole I've dated. Not anymore. I take a deep breath, smiling in the mirror. I spend the next minutes fiddling with some tissues, trying to clean off the stain, then give up, pushing my chest forward instead. I can't hide the damn stain. I can use it to my advantage. And some advantage it gives me. A neon sign couldn't attract more attention to my cleavage, and I don't need this kind of attention right now. I decide to use the dress as an excuse to leave early. To my dismay, Parker is leaning against the wall farther down the corridor, one or two turns away from the entrance to the bar. His eyes rest on the stain on my dress for a few seconds and my cheeks flare up instantly. I'm sure he can see the redness in them even in the dim light.

"I have to go," I say. "My dress is soaked."

"I'll drive you home," he says, walking toward me.

"No, you just got here. I'm sure you and Dani have lots to talk about." I actually take a step back, only to hit the wall behind me.

"I'd just drop you off and return. Are you afraid of being alone with me, Jessica?"

"No . . . it's just not necessary. I can take a cab."

"What are you afraid of?" he insists, stepping right in front of me. "That I'll try to seduce you and take you to bed? Do I really strike you like that kind of guy?"

In my experience, men who don't look even half as godlike as he does are after one thing only. But his rejection all those months ago proves he isn't one of them. And nothing I've seen or heard about him indicated he's a womanizer. But being so close to him makes it impossible to think rationally.

I push him away, but with one swing, he grabs both my hands and pins them against the wall above me. His lips are inches away from mine, the fingers of his free hand tracing the contour of my lips, leaving a trail of fire behind them. He's so close to me that I can feel every single hot breath against my lips. He locks eyes with me, and it's the sight of his blue eyes boring into mine—more than his proximity and his touch—that sets me on fire, causing an almost unbearable pressure between my thighs.

He trails his fingers from my lips down to my chin and then slowly over my neck. I bite my lip when he presses gently with his thumb on the hollow of my neck, then proceeds with his torture farther down. His fingers peruse the hem of my neckline, at the exact point where the soaked fabric of the dress meets my skin, then slip under the fabric. Just a fraction of an inch.

Not enough to actually touch my breast.

But more than enough to send me over the edge. *He's going to kiss me.*

The corners of his lips lift in a delicious smile as he removes his hand from my neckline, letting it fall by his side. His eyes never leave mine. I wait, sucking in my breath, for him to lean forward and kiss me. After what feels like hours, he finally leans forward and kisses me.

On my goddamn forehead.

He walks me out of the club in silence. While he hails me a cab, I run my hands up and down. The wet spot clings to my skin, making me shiver despite the warm end of July evening. Once a car pulls over, I climb in quickly, waving at him. When I arrive at the apartment I share with Dani, I get rid of the wet dress, then slip under the covers.

I'm playing with my phone, looking at cat pictures on Instagram, when a message from Parker pops up.

Parker: Made it home alright?

I like that he's checking in with me.

Jess: Yes.

Parker: Don't be a stranger.

Jess: Please elaborate.

I hover with my fingers above the screen before pressing send, then add a smiley face.

Parker: You're still upset about what happened back in the States, aren't you?

Well, yep. I don't know what to write back, so I just stare at the screen, until another message pops up.

Parker: It wasn't your fault. It's all on me. Trust me, it's better this way.

Right…this isn't making me *feel* better.

Parker: Peace?

I smile, because I wasn't expecting him to wave a white flag. But months have passed since that incident, and we're bound to see each other soon. I don't want Dani to be uncomfortable.

Jess: Okay. Have fun with Dani. I'm going to go to sleep.

Parker: Sweet dreams, Jess.

95183923R00190

Made in the USA
Columbia, SC
07 May 2018